D0048891

TRAPPED IN SPACE

by Jack Williamson

Illustrated by Robert Amundsen

SCHOLASTIC BOOK SERVICES

NEW YORK • TORONTO • LONDON • AUCKLAND • SYDNEY

Copyright © 1968 by Doubleday & Company, Inc. This edition is published by Scholastic Book Services, a division of Scholastic Magazines, Inc., by arrangement with Doubleday & Company, Inc.

1st printing .... October 1970

Printed in the U.S.A.

CONTENTS

STARMEN LOST!

Jeff Stone looked up from left field.

"Three . . . two . . . one. . . ."

He finished the countdown in his head and eyed the sunny sky beyond the baseball park. First he saw a white cotton ball of cloud and then a jet plane floating down to land. The rocket taking off for the moon was late.

There it was! A distant spark of bright metal, it climbed fast on its own leaning tower of cloud. Jeff let out his breath. Like a little boy watching a candy machine but needing a dime, he stood dreaming about space and the starships and his brother Ben.

Ben was older than Jeff, already twenty and a starship pilot. He had left the moon in his tiny four-man ship just six weeks ago to find the planets of a new star.

Jeff was two years behind Ben, but now his own class had finished pilot training at Space School. He was a starman now, at home on a ten-day leave, waiting for his orders — waiting for his chance to catch up.

He had always been waiting. Ben had always been far ahead, not just in years. Ben was handsome, with fine blue eyes, curly hair, and a quick smile. Jeff was skinny and sometimes clumsy, always seeming to try too hard. He'd had to struggle for his marks, while Ben had easily led his class. Jeff had just made the baseball and basketball teams, while Ben was an athletic star.

Out in space, Jeff thought, things might be somehow different —

Crack!

The sharp sound of bat against ball brought him back to the game. He saw the batter racing toward first and the ball in the air. He looked once at the ball and headed toward the spot where it would come down.

"Keep your eye on the ball!" the third baseman hissed at him.

But Jeff didn't need to watch it. A ball in flight was like a ship in space. That was something he had learned in pilot training. A pilot had to have a sense of mass and force and motion. He got into position under the ball and reached up with his glove.

"Watch it, Jeff — "

The ball thudded into his glove.

The third baseman grinned at him as they walked off the field.

"Okay, Jeff! You sure make it look easy."

Jeff didn't say that catching a ball was something like steering a starship to land on a planet. These were old friends he had known before he had gone to Space School. The game was to welcome him home. He didn't want to show off — not too much.

"It's just an old trick of Ben's," he said. Then he saw his mother coming toward them and hurried to meet her.

Her face looked gray and her hands were shaking.

"Bad news, Jeff." Her voice was a dry whisper. "Ben's probe is missing."

Jeff felt as sick as his mother looked. He took her home and she gave him the tape the ferry had brought from the moon.

"It's from the admiral," she said. "Admiral Serov himself."

"He's like that," Jeff said. "They raised his rank because his job is so important, but he still tries to take care of everything. He worries about every man and every probe."

At last, Jeff's numb fingers got the tape in place and he started the player.

"To the parents of Starman Ben Stone — "

The admiral's voice sounded solemn, and Jeff could hear the pain in it.

"I regret to inform you that your son is reported missing in space. He was the pilot of Flight A, which left the moon six weeks ago to explore the planets of the new star Topaz. His flight is now two weeks past due and there has been no report from Flight A.

"The Star Service is grateful to Starman Ben Stone for all he has done, and grateful to his family for their sacrifice — "

His mother turned the player off. "I don't know what went wrong with my two boys." She sighed. "You both always seemed to be trying to break your silly necks, and now . . ."

Her voice broke and she began to sob softly.

Jeff waited until his mother's crying stopped. Then he tried to explain, as Ben had tried before.

"But these starship voyages are important. We must know more about our world. Pilots like Ben have to take their chances."

His mother's lips were set tight. He knew he wasn't getting through.

"Of course the voyages are dangerous," he continued. "Ben knew that. Every flight is a risk. The stars are so far off we can't see their planets — if they have planets. We never know what we will find."

His mother's tired nod meant little.

"A third of our star voyages never come back," he told her. "Ben knew that. But he went anyhow."

"Why — " She choked. "Why did Ben go?"

"Because he's a pilot," Jeff said. "We talked about it while he was home. If one star voyage is lost, another goes out to make up for the loss."

His own eagerness began to wash away his worry.

"That's why we fly to the stars, Mom. Sure, some don't come back. But the lucky ones open the way to new planets — to new worlds for millions of people. That's why Ben went out."

"Can't they send a rescue ship?"

Of course! A rescue ship! It was not always possible, Jeff knew. But maybe his mother had something. "Let me call the moon base, Mom. Maybe there can be a rescue voyage."

Jeff stepped to the TV telephone screen. He had to wait for a channel to the moon. He was afraid, really, of what the answer would be. Rescue ships were seldom sent. But Ben was his own brother. Perhaps, if Jeff himself were to pilot . . .

A blue-green mark on the screen warned Jeff that the moon beam was coming through.

The picture of Space Admiral Serov came on the phone screen. He had been a pilot once, and he wore an empty sleeve. He had lost an arm in a star voyage accident. Even on the laser beam, Jeff's voice took more than a second to reach the moon. The reply took as long to come back. Jeff felt nervous.

"Sir, this is star pilot Jeff Stone. I ask permission to fly a rescue voyage to find Flight A — the men lost on the Topaz flight."

9

Waiting, Jeff heard his mother cry out, "No, Jeff!"

The admiral's voice came back from the moon. "Request denied."

"But — sir!" Jeff caught his breath. "Starman Ben Stone is my brother."

The admiral's face came alive on the screen. "Sorry, Stone." His voice turned softer. "You and your parents have my personal sympathy. But you know the reasons why we can't try a rescue."

The admiral paused, as if finished, but then continued. Jeff knew what he would say.

"One reason is official policy. At one time we did send rescue voyages. We have found that the odds are too great. We have no ships or starmen to waste."

"Admiral — "

The admiral didn't wait for Jeff. "Here's the other reason. We have no starship ready. Your brother flew the last SP-9 in service. The new SP-12 won't be ready in time for a rescue flight."

For a moment, Jeff felt hope. "But, sir, we do have a ship!" Excitement lifted his voice. "The old SP-7 training ship. The one I flew at Space School to earn my rating. It was built for star flights. Let me take it to Topaz!"

The admiral frowned, shaking his head.

"The ship is out of date," he said. "It lacks proper power and control for X-space flight. It might take you to Topaz, but it probably would not get you back. Request denied."

"Sir — " But the hope was gone.

"Sorry, Starman Stone," the admiral said. "Tell your parents I am truly sorry."

The screen went blank.

"I didn't mean for you to go." His mother's face was white. "I don't want that."

"I know, Mom," Jeff said quietly. "But I am going sometime, and what better time than now?"

Mrs. Stone put her arm around him. Jeff could feel her thin body trembling, and he knew she would never understand. He felt sorry for her, more than for Ben.

A few moments later, when Jeff's father got home, they again played the tape from the moon, and watched the news on the big 3-D screen across the end of the room, showing a film of Ben and his men the way they had looked on the moon, ready for the flight. They were all in their silver uniforms, with the silver needles crossed over their hearts. They grinned and waved before climbing into the slim bright starship.

Jeff recognized them all. They had been Ben's friends at school — and his friends, too. Jim Ozaki had taught him boxing. Tony Mescalero had played cards with him. Whiz Miller had taught him to field and helped him make the baseball team.

On film, Ben waved again and sealed the air lock. The starship was ready to go. A newsman's face came on the screen.

"That was their last good-bye," he said. "They flew from the moon to the X-space station, a million miles out. There they shifted into X-space drive, which is faster than light. Their goal was Topaz — a star so far from Earth that its light takes a thousand years to reach us."

The newsman paused, looking very solemn.

"They gladly risked their lives to win the planets of Topaz for us — if Topaz has any planets. They gambled, and lost. No rescue effort can be made."

Jeff felt relieved when the newsman stopped. His mother cried again. He left his parents sitting together in the living room, and went back to his room — the room he had once shared with Ben.

Ben's bed was there, by the tall glass case their father had built to hold Ben's prizes. The ribbons and cups he had won in swimming, in tennis, and golf. The silver key for high grades.

Jeff stood at the door a long time, just looking at those honors. He remembered all the bitter moments when Ben had beaten him. Sometimes he had hated Ben for being so good at everything — and for being so modest about how good he was, as if it really didn't matter. Now he was ashamed.

"Jeff!" His father was calling. "On the 3-D! News about Ben!"

" — Captain Marc Bon," a newsman was saying. "Captain Bon is in charge of Sun Point, the space station where Ben Stone began his X-space flight to

Topaz. Captain Bon has a message from Starman Stone."

Captain Bon came on the screen. He wore the crossed silver needles of a star pilot.

"A radio message?" the newsman asked.

"There's no radio between the stars," Captain Bon told the newsman sharply. "If there were, a signal from the star we call Topaz would take a thousand years to get here."

"But you did get a message?"

"In a space capsule," the captain said, "that came back through X-space. The capsule had been partly fused and the message inside was partly destroyed. We can read only a few words."

"And what are those words, captain?"

"Queer kinds of life here . . ." Captain Bon read slowly from a paper in his big brown hand. "Surprise attack . . . things we thought were friendly . . . call them rock hoppers . . . station now under laser fire . . ."

Captain Bon lowered the piece of paper. "That's all we can read. The rest of the message is too burned."

"What's a rock hopper?" the newsman asked.

"Nobody knows," the captain said.

"What does this mean? What will the Star Service do?"

"I don't know what the service can do." The captain frowned. "If the X-space station was destroyed, it means that Starman Stone can't leave Topaz. We have no more ships that can get there. Not till the new SP-12's are ready."

"Jeff!" He heard his mother calling. "Come talk to the moon."

Admiral Serov could be seen on the phone screen.

"Starman Stone," the admiral said, "have you heard about the message from your brother?"

Jeff quickly answered that he had.

The admiral continued. "His report has changed our decision against rescue flights. We see a danger that the queer kinds of life your brother reported may come back through X-space to harm Earth.

"Because of this report," the admiral went on, "we are acting on your idea that the old SP-7 training ship could make the flight to Topaz. A crew has already been picked for it. You are on the list."

Jeff could not quite believe what he heard.

"These orders are official, Starman Stone," the admiral continued. "You will take the next ferry to the moon and report at once to the base here."

STRANGE BEING

JEFF'S PARENTS went with him to the moon ferry. His father talked rapidly, asking question after question about the star flight. Jeff's mother remained silent.

A screaming sound pierced the quiet of the summer air. "Air-raid alarm," Jeff announced to his parents. "Just a practice."

The air taxi they were in lowered itself quickly to the ground. Jeff and his parents ran into a shelter, already filled with people.

Air-raid alarms were quite frequent and Jeff, while in training, had even controlled one of them. The reason for them was that the X-space stations the starmen opened in space, were two-way doors. Voyages went out through them to find new worlds. Bigger ships followed to open space commerce. But there was always the danger that strange things from unknown worlds might try to break through the stations from the other side.

In spite of all the people in the shelter, it was terribly quiet. Then it came, as it always did — the all-clear horn.

Jeff and his parents hurried back to the cab to go to the moon station. The ferry was due to lift in only twenty minutes. Jeff gripped his father's hand and kissed his mother quickly.

"Jeff, we are both proud of you — proud you are going," his mother said.

When the taxi carrying his parents had slid away on its pad of whispering air, Jeff began to feel better. Now he had his job to do. He ran for the passenger gate.

"Hey, you, starman!" The hoarse shout came after him. "What do I do with this thing?"

Jeff looked back. Another air taxi was floating at the curb. The cabman spilled out of it as if he were trying to walk on the air.

"Hey, starman!" His loud voice was thick. "How about some help?"

Jeff walked back, staring at the passenger in the cab. It looked a little like a starved child, and a little like a blown-up spider. It had a round black stomach and thin black limbs covered with fur, and it was buzzing like a queer electric toy.

The cabman staggered to meet Jeff. "I wasn't expecting this for a fare, when they called me to the Space Life Center. I wouldn't have taken it, but a cop put it in my cab and told me somebody would meet it here."

"I can't help you," Jeff said. "I'm already late. Maybe I can find somebody at the ferry station who knows what this is all about."

Yet he felt sorry for the thing in the cab. It lay back in the seat as if Earth's pull were too strong for it. Its eyes were huge. When Jeff moved to go, it buzzed at him weakly.

He knew it was a space alien — a creature that did not belong on Earth. It must have come from one of the new planets. Star voyages often brought back strange life. Aliens had much to offer in the way of scientific knowledge, and almost all of them were friendly and helpful. Jeff thought of those "queer kinds of life" that had attacked Ben. But this creature didn't look as though it would harm anyone.

The cabman hauled it roughly out of the seat and tried to stand it up. Its thin limbs folded and it fell to the pavement, still buzzing.

"I want my fare." The cabman came back to Jeff. "It has no money. And no friends either, so far as I can see. Not after that raid alert."

Jeff knew that many people didn't trust aliens and stayed away from them. He wondered how long it would be before they were accepted on Earth.

The ferry was due to lift. The gates would soon be closing. Jeff didn't know the alien, and he had no time to waste. But he couldn't make himself leave the helpless creature.

"Here's the fare," Jeff said.

The cabman took his money and roughly set the alien's baggage on the pavement. The baggage was something that looked like a huge brown cocoon, a foot thick and a yard long. As the cab roared away, the alien buzzed faintly, pointing a thin arm at the cocoon.

Jeff bent over the buzzing thing. "How can I help you?" he asked. "What can I do?"

The only answer was more buzzing.

He thought it must be hurt or sick, but he had no idea what it needed. The buzzing meant nothing to him. He looked around for the person who was to meet the alien, and saw no one. He decided to look for a policeman.

As he turned, the creature whistled sharply. Its great eyes looked up at him and back at the hollow cocoon. It twisted like a broken bird on the pavement, dragging itself a little way toward the cocoon. Maybe that was what it wanted.

Jeff rolled the cocoon toward it.

It made an eager little hum. Its huge eyes blinked and turned a pale gold color. Its thin, three-fingered hands reached for the cocoon. With Jeff helping, as gently as he could, it scrambled inside. Its lean limbs folded to fit the narrow space. Only the crown of its odd head stuck out, closing the cocoon. Its buzz became a sleepy song, like the purr of a happy cat.

Jeff stood up, feeling rather foolish. The ferry would lift in eleven minutes. The gates would close

in one minute. He wondered what the admiral would say if he tried to explain that he had missed the ferry because he had stopped to help such a strange being.

"Buzz!" A girl's voice called behind him. "Are you all right?"

Another air taxi was sliding toward the curb. A slim girl jumped out and ran to the cocoon. She knelt over it, buzzing like a second electric toy.

The creature's head popped out of the cocoon. Brighter gold, its huge eyes shone up at her.

"I'm terribly sorry to be late." Her quick dark eyes looked up at Jeff. "I got caught in the space-raid alert. So did Buzz. It was dreadful for him."

Gently she stroked the fuzzy head that was looking out of the cocoon.

"Our cabman left him out on the street in the alert. In the confusion we were separated. He doesn't understand much English and he must have felt the force of people's fear and hate during the raid. It must have nearly killed him."

The creature purred again. Its big eyes looked back at Jeff. Now they glowed with warm sparks of green and gold.

"Buzz wants to thank you." A smile flashed across the girl's lean face. "And I do, too. Buzz was — "

"I'm glad you got here," Jeff broke in. "I have to go."

The gates had already closed. Now he could hear the first dull roar as the ferry built up power. High over the station, a thin mist formed and whirled inside the tube of force that was sweeping out a path through the air for the machine.

Seven minutes! Maybe they wouldn't open the gate for him. But at least he could try. He grabbed his light space bag and started running toward the gates.

"Wait — please!" the girl called after him. "We are going, too. Buzz says he will tell them to open the gates. He says they'll open the locks and hold the ferry five minutes for us. No time to explain — but you must help me carry Buzz!"

Jeff ran on for half a second, wondering what she meant. How could Buzz tell them to open the gates? Why would they hold the ferry? But then he saw the gates sliding open for them.

He came back and picked up the brown cocoon. It felt lighter than it looked. He swung it to his shoulder like a roll of carpet. The girl slipped the space bag off his arm.

"Thanks!" she said. "Let me carry this."

He trotted toward the gates, the girl running beside him, buzzing. The cocoon buzzed back.

"Later!" she gasped at Jeff. "Later — we will explain."

The air lock into the ferry was open. Reaching hands hauled Jeff through it and took the cocoon. In another ninety seconds he was in his tiny cabin, lying back in the padded shock seat.

The launch field was roaring again, like a storm far away. Horns hooted. Jeff felt the shock, like something exploding under him. The ferry rose, putting pressure on Jeff so that soon he weighed half a ton.

The thrust seemed to go on forever, squeezing his body and dragging at his brain. He could hardly breathe.

When the main jets changed to the gentle push of the boosters, he felt too dull to think. He wanted to find the girl and talk to her about the queer little alien, but the seat was too comfortable. Perhaps the flight shot had made him sleepy. . . .

When he woke, the ferry was falling toward the moon. He washed his face, brushed his uniform and went out on deck. The passenger deck had no real windows, but a big screen showed their approach.

The moon was swelling in that screen as they fell. It was a big bright ball against the dusty dark of space. He could see the wrinkled mountains and the round holes where shadows lay like puddles of ink.

Sickness hit the pit of his stomach.

Jeff felt ashamed, and angry at himself, and a little afraid. The truth was, heights had frightened him since he was very young. He had no idea why.

His brother Ben had climbed everything, their mother said, since he began to crawl — boxes and chairs and cabinet drawers. Later, it was trees and walls and even flagpoles. Jeff had always tried to follow Ben, and he had always been afraid.

He had never talked about it, not even to Ben, but he had tried to fight that fear. At school he had tried high diving. He had practiced on the flying rings. But still he had been afraid.

Half the reason he had followed Ben through pilot training was to beat this old enemy. He had not beaten it entirely, but he had learned to keep it under control.

Most of the training hadn't been so bad, because it was on the ground. Even most of the training flights were in model spaceships, with 3-D screens to show the look of space. Real flight was not so easy.

His flight alone in the old SP-7 had left him weak and cold and dripping sweat. But at least he knew he had faced his fear at its worst and come out all right. It would never be so bad again.

Jeff tried not to look at the moon in the screen, but he couldn't pull his eyes away. The moon was a great sharp ball of rock; its face scarred and terrible. He waited for the strong retro jets that would catch the ferry and steer it into the landing net. All he could feel was the gentle thrust of the boosters, too weak to stop that ten-thousand-mile fall.

"Excuse me, Starman Stone." A lean little man had touched his arm. "We are with the Space News Service." He waved toward a short, fat man with a camera. "Will you speak to our 3-D audience?"

Jeff felt nervous in front of the camera, but he was glad to have something else to think about.

"Tell us about the starships," the newsman said. "What are they like?"

"They are the smallest spaceships," Jeff said. "And

the fastest. They are used to discover the world of new stars. They can do this because they have X-space drive."

"Will you explain X-space flight for our viewers?"

Jeff thought hard, trying to make it clear.

"In ordinary space," he said, "the speed of light is the limit. Light seems fast — it goes 186,000 miles a second. But that's too slow for trips to the stars. Most trips would take hundreds of years at that rate. In X-space flight, we break the speed limit."

The lump was still in his stomach, but Jeff tried to grin, aware of the camera.

"The X-space drive twists each atom partly out of common space," he continued. "The mass of each atom drops toward zero. As mass goes down, speed goes up. A starship can make a thousand light-years in ten hours."

He looked at the camera, explaining that, "One light-year is the distance light can go in one year. It's nearly six trillion miles."

"What makes X-space so dangerous?"

Jeff shook his head. "It isn't. You are safe in X-space flight. The risk is all in ordinary space, when you come back out of X-space drive."

"Why so?"

"You come out fast," Jeff said. "Too fast to see what's ahead. Too fast for your instruments to be much help. You have to depend on yourself and your team — "

He stopped, hoping good men had been picked to go with him on the Topaz flight.

"You have to be extremely alert. There are so many objects in space that could smash your ship to bits if not avoided."

"How about the X-space ships? Are they dangerous?"

"Not a bit," Jeff said. "You see, the voyages carry an X-space station to each new star. The station has a beacon that guides arriving ships past any danger. Coming and going through the station, the big ships are as safe as this ferry."

"Thank you, Starman Stone. We wish you luck on your rescue flight to Topaz."

The newsman turned from Jeff to the 3-D camera.

"That was Starman Jefferson Stone. He will be on the Topaz rescue flight. Now I see two other crew members that you will want to meet."

He hurried off across the deck, the fat cameraman behind him. Jeff followed, eager to see who would be with him on the rescue flight.

" — Lupe Flor," the newsman was saying. "She's an official starman. So is her friend here. They were picked as members of the Topaz rescue team, to go along with Starman Stone."

Jeff walked over to the ring of passengers standing by. Lupe Flor, he saw, was the slim dark girl who had come aboard the ferry with him. And her "friend" was the fuzzy little space alien!

MOONQUAKE!

THE SCARRED gray curve of the moon filled the big screen. And still the ferry fell.

Jeff watched the screen, listening for the jets that ought to be catching the falling ferry, thinking about the two strange members of his crew. A girl and a fuzzy alien — they couldn't be much good on the rescue flight. To find and help Ben, he needed trained men. The girl and the strange being were half the cause of the knot in his stomach.

"Thank you, Lupe Flor," he heard the newsman say. "Now will you introduce your friend?"

Jeff slipped into the ring of people around them.

"I call him Buzz Dozen-Dozen."

Lupe Flor smiled down at the purring alien. Out of the cocoon, he looked different now. His short fur had turned bright blue. Even his saucer eyes were blue now, happily watching Lupe.

"He has no real name," she told the newsman. "You see, he's not a separate person. Not like one of us. He's part of a multiple being, and he doesn't need a name when he's at home. The number on his space passport ends with 1212 — that's where we got the Dozen-Dozen."

The newsman looked at Lupe. "Would you explain a multiple being?"

"It's made of millions of parts," Lupe said. "Just as our own bodies are made of millions of cells. They all work together for each other. Each brother-sister, sister-brother has a body like Buzz's and all the parts think together."

"How do you mean?"

"They all belong to one great mind," she said. "Buzz has his own brain cells. So does each brother-sister. But the mastermind of the multiple being links them all together. Look at Buzz."

She touched his thin blue arm, and the newsman made a quick signal for the camera to pick him up.

"His body is here with us, but his mind is linked to all his brother-sisters everywhere — most of them are still on the worlds of Opal, his home star. The links work faster than X-space flight. Distance doesn't matter. The multiple mind can see and speak and act through any brother-sister."

The little alien purred at her and gave a solemn nod, as if it understood.

"Here's an example," she said. "Back on Earth, we were delayed by a space-raid alert. The ferry was about to leave us. But Buzz has a sister-brother at the moon base. That sister-brother knew all about our trouble on Earth. Buzz sent her his message and had the ferry held for us."

So that was it, Jeff thought. He began to realize that Buzz could be pretty useful.

The newsman was saying, "Starman Flor, will you tell us how you met Buzz?"

"Buzz is my own brother-sister," Lupe said. "I've known him all my life. You see, my father and mother were starmen. They came from Puerto Rico, and they were on the first voyage to Opal — which is two thousand light-years beyond the North Star.

"Coming out of X-space flight, their ship hit a grain of dust. My father was the pilot. The ship was crippled and he was hurt. He lived just long enough to land on the nearest planet of Opal."

The newsman looked at Lupe with sympathy.

"But I was lucky." Lupe's dark eyes shone. "The planets of Opal belong to the multiple being. Buzz's bigger brother-sisters pulled my mother out of the wreck. She had been hurt terribly, but she lived until I was born.

"The multiple being took care of me. Buzz became my special brother-sister. He played with me and taught me and grew up with me. Finally his brother-sisters made a little X-spaceship, patterned partly after the wreck of the old starship, and Buzz came on it with me to look for my own people."

Smiling down at the little blue alien, she made a purring sound.

"And here we are!"

"Thank you, Lupe Flor," the newsman said. "That's a wonderful story. Now there's one more thing I want to ask you."

"Yes?"

"This rescue flight will be dangerous," the newsman said. "It calls for expert starmen. Why do you think you and Buzz were picked?"

"In the first place," Lupe answered seriously, "there aren't many star pilots. Only a few men pass the entrance tests. Most of them wash out before they finish training. Those who finish make only three voyages on the average. So I didn't have that much competition.

"I do know why Buzz was picked."

Jeff listened carefully. This was what he had to know.

"He will be a kind of living telephone." Gently, Lupe was stroking his bright blue fur. "Our signals can't reach the distant stars, but Buzz will always be in instant touch with his sister-brother at the base on the moon."

"Is that important?"

"It will be important," Lupe said, "if we run into trouble. In the past, when a starship was lost, nobody knew why. Too many rescue voyages have failed to come back because their crews repeated the same mistake. This time we can file a running report to the base on the moon. If we make mistakes, the admiral will know what they are. If we don't come back, the people in the next voyage will know what went wrong."

"That makes sense." The newsman nodded. "In the long run, anyhow. Though I don't see how it can save your voyage. Or how it can help Ben Stone and his starmen."

"Other ships will follow us," Lupe said. "If they can't come in time to help us, it is still our job to clear the way to new stars."

"I'm sure our viewers will want to know how a girl happened to be picked for this flight," the newsman said. "You never really explained that."

"For one thing — " Lupe hesitated before going on. "Well, I'm pretty good at getting around in space, though I don't use the human system. You see, Buzz's brother-sisters taught me a lot of their own sort of science while I was growing up on the worlds of Opal."

"Oh." The newsman looked surprised.

"For another thing," Lupe said, "I guess it was known that Buzz needs me."

"Why is that?" the newsman asked.

"Buzz can't speak human sounds, and most people can't understand him. Lots of people don't like him — I can't see why."

Buzz purred at her and gripped her finger with a small blue hand.

"We were separated in that space-raid alert," she

31

said. "People ran from Buzz, because he's a space alien. Their fear and hate hurt him terribly. He was nearly dead when Starman Stone rescued him and helped him back into his cocoon."

She saw Jeff across the deck and smiled at him.

"We are both glad Starman Stone will be with us on the rescue voyage."

The 3-D camera swung to Jeff.

"Now I have a question for all three of you," the newsman said. He motioned for Jeff to stand with Lupe and Buzz.

"How do you plan to deal with the rock hoppers of Topaz — I think that's what the distress message called them?" He looked at Buzz. "How about you, Starman Dozen-Dozen? How can you fight the rock hoppers?"

Buzz shook his head and made a low sound.

"The multiple being is not a fighting creature," Lupe said. "It doesn't believe in war. Buzz says he will try to make peace with the hoppers when we meet them."

"Suppose they don't want peace?" the newsman asked. "How will you defend yourself, Starman Flor?"

"I grew up with Buzz," Lupe said. "I don't like fighting any better than he does. I believe that space is big enough for all creatures. I will work with Buzz for peace."

The newsman turned to Jeff.

"How about you, Starman Stone?"

"I'm not looking for trouble," Jeff said. "But the

pilot of the lost voyage was my brother. I'm going to help him in any way I can."

"So you are prepared to fight?"

"The starships are not armed," Jeff said. "They're too small to carry heavy weapons. But I will want permission to carry weapons on the rescue flight. If necessary, I will fight with everything I have."

A horn honked.

"Shock seats, please," a loud voice ordered through a speaker. "Prepare to land on the moon. Shock seats, everybody."

The newsman waved to Lupe and Buzz and Jeff. "Thank you all and good luck on your rescue flight." He made a sign to the fat man with the camera. "This is Space News — "

The horn was honking again. Jeff hurried back to the shock seat in his tiny cabin. Though he was still worried about having Buzz and Lupe on his crew, at least the cold knot was gone from his stomach.

His blood raced with a new excitement. They were landing on the moon. The old SP-7 should be waiting for them there. Who else, he wondered, had been picked for the crew?

The hard thrust of the jets braked the ferry. Jeff left his seat, grabbed his space bag, and scrambled out of the cabin. He saw Lupe and Buzz just ahead of him. Eagerly, he looked around the ferry station. It was a huge round room, dug deep in the moon and walled with bare concrete. The ferry was a tall silver tower standing in the middle of it.

Electric trucks moved rapidly over the floor. Loud speakers boomed. High overhead, humming machines carried freight and baggage off the ferry.

"Hi, Jeff!"

The happy shout came from among the waiting crowd. A tall spaceman ran over to meet him.

"Hi, Tiger!"

Jeff pounded his friend, Ty Clark's back. The slim black man looked lean and handsome in his silver uniform.

"I guess we are going to be together on the Topaz job!"

"We are?" If Ty Clark was a crew member, Jeff was delighted. Ty was good at everything. He had been commander of the new boys at Space School and champion of the class in boxing.

"I've got our orders here." Ty showed him a gray official envelope. "I've been picked for pilot. You are co-pilot. I'm looking for the rest of our crew."

Jeff felt a stab of disappointment. He had half expected to be pilot of the rescue voyage. He had wanted to be the one in charge of rescuing Ben.

But then he felt ashamed of himself. Topaz A had to be rescued. Nothing else really mattered. The best available pilot had to be picked, and of course that was Ty.

He wondered for a second if his own weakness was known. But he decided that wasn't likely. His fear of high places couldn't be that serious or the tests he had taken would have washed him out of Space School.

He was lucky, he thought, even to be assistant pilot. It took a moment for him to pull himself together. Then he looked back into Ty's smiling face.

"I'm glad I can work with you, Ty!" Jeff told him warmly. "Our other starmen are just ahead."

He called Lupe and Buzz — and waited to see how Ty would act. But Ty didn't even seem surprised that the other members of the rescue team were going to be a girl and a little, blue, alien being.

"This is Tyler Clark," Jeff told them. "Back at Space School, we used to call him the smiling tiger. He was my roommate there, and the best friend I had. He will be our pilot to Topaz."

In his easy, friendly way, Ty shook hands with Lupe and Buzz.

"We have to fly a training ship, because it's all there is," he told them. "It needs repairs, but we will take off as soon as the ship is ready."

He nodded toward the passenger lanes.

"Come on," he said. "I've got a moon car from the base. We can go right out there and stand by for the Topaz flight."

Jeff started for the lanes, walking carefully. His weight here was only thirty pounds. Anyone who forgot bounced off the floor.

"Don't lift your feet," Ty said.

"Wait," Lupe called to him. "We've got baggage to pick up."

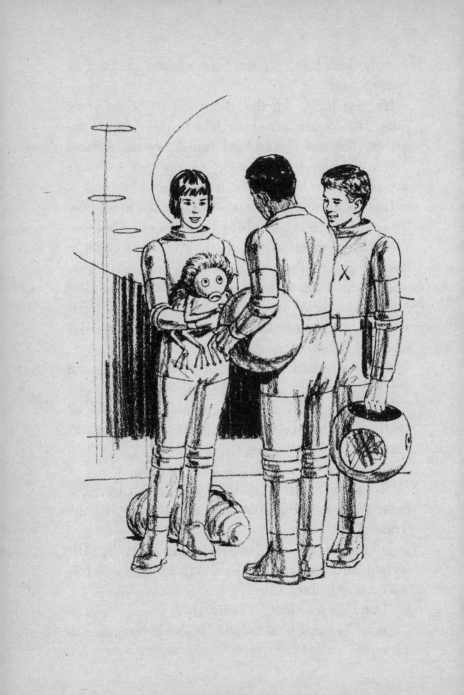

"Better forget it," Ty told her. "Our old ship has scarcely enough power for X-space flight as it is. They're stripping every possible ounce off it now. We can't carry any extras."

Buzz whined and pulled at her finger, blinking back toward the ferry.

"He's worried about his cocoon," she said. "He's got to have it, to help him link up with all his brother-sisters. We can't go without it — "

Jeff felt a shaking under his feet. Lupe's voice was drowned in a rumble of thunder that seemed to come from deep in the moon. The tall ferry swayed back and forth. Gongs clanged. Men shouted and ducked and ran. A truck without a driver crashed into the passenger lanes.

All these sounds bellowed back again from the gloomy dome over their heads, until Jeff had to put his fingers in his ears. He looked for his friends and saw Buzz falling down between Lupe and Ty. The blue glow had faded from his eyes and his fur, leaving him black all over.

"Moonquake!" A frightened man stumbled past them, staring high into that roaring dome. "Get out!"

Jeff looked up in time to see a machine break free from the swaying ferry. It dropped, moving slowly at first and then picking up speed, its heavy load of crates and trunks and metal drums raining down toward the passenger lanes from a hundred feet above.

"Let's go!" Ty nodded at Jeff and caught Lupe's hand. "Scramble!"

TAKEOFF FOR TOPAZ

JEFF STARED UP at the space cargo spilling off the broken machine. The motion of the tumbling crates and drums here on the moon was strange to him. Everything seemed to fall slowly at first, then to come down with a rush. It took him a moment to get the feel of the mass and force and motion. Then he knew exactly when each spinning crate would crash to the station floor. And he knew exactly where.

"Jeff!" Ty Clark caught his arm. "Move!"

Lupe was bending over Buzz. The little space alien lay limp on the floor.

"Come on, starman." Ty scooped up Buzz. "I can carry him."

He plunged toward the exit, Lupe close behind him. Jeff stood frozen for half a second. They were running right under the falling cargo!

"Tiger!" he shouted. "Hold it!"

"Huh?" Ty swung around. "We've no time — "

"Crates." Jeff pointed ahead. "Safer here."

Ty glanced up at the falling freight, a grin on his face, as if moonquakes were great fun.

"You are on the passenger lane!" Jeff shouted at the frightened people beyond. "Get off."

Ty ran up with Buzz in his arms and Lupe close behind.

"Right here!" Jeff pointed. "Don't move — "

Crash!

Twenty feet from where they stood, a big crate of equipment hit the ground in a shower of flashing metal and glass. A string of heavy trunks exploded. A thick metal drum flattened on the floor beyond, spotting screaming people with bright yellow paint.

And then the quake was over. Men ran to pick up three or four people who had been hurt. A passenger gathered up his wife and children and came panting to thank Jeff for warning them.

The alarm stopped wailing. Workmen came back to clean up the mess and to finish taking cargo off the ferry. Soon the high dome boomed again, with the sound of normal work.

Buzz was humming weakly, and a pale gold gleam shone again from his eyes and the tips of his fur. Ty set him back on the floor.

"Thanks, Jeff!" Ty grinned. "Just for a second, I thought you were crazy. Then I remembered watching you catch high fly balls."

"We want to thank you, too," Lupe said. "I guess you saved our lives!"

"Things fall slowly here." Jeff explained, trying not to show how the accident had shaken him. "They took six seconds to reach the floor from that machine. I had time enough to see where they would hit."

They collected Buzz's cocoon and then walked down a parking tunnel to the moon car. It looked like a high-wheeled tank truck. They climbed through an air lock at the rear, and Ty drove them through a web of dim tunnels.

The moon colonies had been built underground for protection against the long burning days and long bitter nights. Even the road out to the starship base was sheltered most of the way in a deep, covered ditch, but at one point it ran across a long bridge, out beneath the strange dark sky.

Sitting in front with Ty, Jeff looked around at the land, dead and gray under the blaze of the sun and the darkness of space. It was pitted with ugly holes. Rocks like broken teeth stood up everywhere. Jeff wondered if the unknown worlds of Topaz could be as cruel as the moon looked.

Admiral Serov's assistant was waiting for them at the gate of the base. "You are to report to the takeoff area right away," he told them. "Your ship is loading fuel now. You'll take off soon."

The takeoff area was a cone-shaped cave cut out of the moon. The sloping walls were gray concrete. The catapult — the machine used to send the ship on its way — was a heavy black cannon, pointing through the roof. On it was the SP-7.

"That's our ship?" Lupe stared at it.

Jeff nodded. "That's it."

"It looks so tiny."

"The new ships are bigger," Jeff said. "But we don't have a new one. This old training ship is our one chance to rescue Ben and his crew."

The ground crew was swarming over the starship. Admiral Serov had been checking everything out himself, and he came stumping over to meet the starmen, his empty sleeve tucked into his belt. His face wore a worried look, but he smiled at Lupe and hummed at Buzz, whose language he understood, and shook Jeff's hand when he tried to salute.

"You've been briefed for the mission," he said to Ty. "You can go aboard now."

"Yes, sir." Ty hesitated. "About the repairs I asked for — "

"Our crew chief went over your trouble sheet," the admiral said. "We've checked everything out. I know this starship is old, but she still flies."

"But the flight teachers at school never let us push her past half the speed of light," Ty told him. "They said she hadn't been fully tested at high speeds. Doesn't that mean her X-space system hasn't been proved in actual flight?"

"Our crew chief says her instruments all check out," the admiral said. "You'll just have to nurse her along. We don't have time for more tests now."

"I see, sir." Ty nodded. "We will take her as she is."

"Admiral Serov — " Jeff was nervous. "Can we carry any weapons?"

The admiral frowned at him. "You know the policy. Our ships carry peace to the stars, not war."

"But sir," Jeff said, "the creatures of Topaz attacked my brother. How can we defend ourselves?"

"One small starship can't carry weapons to conquer a system of planets," the admiral reminded him. "You could only make the aliens hate you — and perhaps encourage them to attack our worlds."

"I don't see much we can do for Flight Topaz A without weapons," Jeff said. "Ben reported that those hoppers were firing on his X-space station. They probably destroyed it. Suppose they hit our ship or wreck our station? What can we do?"

"You'll have to work that out," the admiral said. "Buzz and Lupe should be able to help you there."

Buzz had turned bright blue again. He whistled at the admiral. The admiral whistled back, in his own language. The ground crew loaded his cocoon into the ship. Other workers scrambled on and off, finishing up the job of getting the starship ready for takeoff.

Jeff walked with Lupe and Buzz and Ty to the platform of an open elevator. The crew chief made a signal, and the platform swung them up toward the open air lock. The ground crew waved.

A signal gong made a hollow boom against the

concrete dome. Ty Clark followed Jeff and Lupe and Buzz into the ship.

The closing lock clanged. There was a roar that sounded like a stiff wind. Great machines lifted the starship into position. High over the moon's face, the ship left the field. With a hot gleam of sun on bright metal, it turned north and headed toward Sun Point — the X-space station that was Earth's gateway to the stars.

Jeff sat beside Ty in the narrow cockpit, trying hard to be as happy as Ty looked. At last they were off to Topaz. With a little mass reduction, they could reach Sun Point in two hours.

Beyond Sun Point, ten hours of X-space flight would take them to Topaz. If they were lucky, they might be there before the moon ferry got back to Earth.

Yet Jeff worried about their ship. If the starships were the fastest things men had ever made, they were also just about the most dangerous to fly. He sat watching the instrument board for signs of trouble.

"What do you think?" he asked Ty. "Will she make it?"

"Sure she will!" Ty bent forward in the pilot's seat, and reached to push the mass-reduction lever farther forward.

But Jeff was not so certain.

"I'm worried about Ben," he said. "Even if we get safely to Topaz, I don't see how we will ever find him — not with maybe a whole swarm of unknown plan-

43

ets to search. And I don't see how we can face those rock hoppers — whatever they are — without weapons."

"No sweat." Ty grinned. "We will fight with what we've got."

Jeff wished he could feel as certain as Ty. Their ship was small and old. And it carried the extra weight of the new station for Topaz that was loaded in the nose cone. The load was heavy. What if it made the ship slow and clumsy, and caused trouble in the dangerous seconds of the cut out from X-space flight?

Yet they had to carry the station. Without it, they couldn't come back from Topaz. Until it was set up and working, flashing its beacon and sweeping out a safe entrance zone, no larger ships could follow them to Topaz.

He worried about Lupe and Buzz, down in the cabin. He liked Lupe. He thought Buzz was wonderful. But still he didn't see how they could take the place of weapons against the rock hoppers of Topaz.

Thrum! . . . Thrum! . . . Thrum! . . .

A hammering movement shook the cockpit. Jeff felt the little ship fall, as if the force that lifted them had failed. He snatched at the controls.

"Easy, Jeff!"

Quickly, Ty cut the thrust of the jets back to zero. The banging stopped. The ship drifted for a moment in free fall. Jeff's body had no weight, and he felt a dizzy sickness.

"Those were the boosters," Ty explained. "Remember, the admiral said to nurse them along."

Jeff nodded weakly. He gripped the straps that held him in the seat and waited while Ty worked with the controls to measure mass and power back into the boosters. He felt a little better when the starship came back to life.

"Flight Topaz B to Sun Point." Ty was beaming a signal to the station north of the moon. "Tyler Clark in command. Have you any news of Flight Topaz A?"

Sun Point was still very far ahead. Even at the speed of light, the deep voice of Captain Marc Bon took quite some time to come back to them.

"No more news," the captain said. "We don't expect any. We are certain that Stone's X-space station was destroyed. He can't send news and he can't come back."

"We are going after him." Ty's cheerful voice turned sharp. "Sir, we request to be cleared through Sun Point, for X-space flight to Topaz."

"Request approved," Bon answered. A moment later, Bon's deep voice gave them their directions. Ty tapped the keys of his flight machine and guided the starship into the entrance zone. He pushed the mass-reduction lever to shift their ship into X-space drive.

"Good luck, starmen!" Bon was calling. "Come back — "

His voice was cut off, because they were moving faster than the beam of light that carried it. The moon and the Earth and the sun disappeared behind them, their rays of light unable to keep pace.

Ty grinned at Jeff. They had studied the theory at school. The flight teachers had let them use the mass-reduction lever to push the old training ship to half the speed of light. Buzz and Lupe, of course, had flown through X-space to Earth. But for Jeff and Ty, actual X-space flight was a new experience.

"They said we couldn't see the stars." Ty looked at the cockpit windows. "Sure enough we can't. They say we can fly right through a star or even a planet."

Ty, leaning toward the glowing instrument board, looked willing to fly through anything. "They say nothing can hurt us, in X-space flight."

"But we can be smashed to pieces," Jeff reminded him, "when we cut out."

"So we take our chances."

Ty reached for the controls. The soft glow of the board shone on his fingers, but there was no light outside the cockpit windows. The ghost world was black.

"This old neutrino scope — " His voice trailed off as he worked the knobs. "Our crew chief says it's okay. If he's wrong, we are blind."

The neutrino scope was an eye for the starship. As he watched Ty working over it, Jeff remembered his courses at school. Neutrinos, he'd learned, were queer tiny bits that had no mass. Most of them were slower than light, but the X-space effect made some of them race faster than the fastest ship.

The cores of stars shone with fast neutrinos. That

47

was the secret of the scope. Though human eyes can't see neutrinos, the scope trapped them in silvered mirrors to show the stars in every direction from the probe.

When it was working, Jeff thought. But it wasn't working now. All the mirrors were empty. Their starship flew through dead darkness.

"Could be, the crew chief is right." Ty shook his head. "Could be, he's wrong. All the lines are getting power. Could be, the scope just needs a little fixing — "

His worried voice died again. Still the mirrors were dark.

Jeff twisted in his seat to look at the little clock on the board. It was measuring distance now, as well as time, for they were flying fast. They had to fly fast to catch neutrinos in the scope. The seconds were hundreds of millions of miles. The minutes were light-years.

Already, he knew, they were flashing past other stars. Their own sun, with its tiny planets moving around it, was already so far behind that it would be hard to pick out.

He watched Ty and waited for the scope to show the stars again. He was breathing too hard. He tried not to look at the clock, but he couldn't keep his eyes off the racing second hand. He couldn't help wondering what would happen if they really hit a planet or a star.

Ty's cheery whistle almost frightened him.

"The chief was right," Ty said. "All it needed was a little fixing."

The mirrors flickered. A pale gray fog spread across them. Gray dots swam out of the fog in the forward mirror. They raced across the side mirrors, passing the ship. In the rear mirror, they faded back into the fog.

That gray fog was made up of all the far-off stars, Jeff knew. The racing dots were the cores of the nearer stars, shining with their fast neutrinos trapped in the mirrors.

"So now we can see!" Jeff drew a deep breath. "I was afraid — "

His voice trailed away.

Ty frowned into the mirrors and shook his head. Finally he looked up at Jeff. His round eyes were serious.

"Trouble, Jeff. Big trouble. I took too long to tune the scope. I don't know where we got to, while we were flying blind. I don't know which direction Topaz is. Or even where our own sun is. We are lost, Jeff. All these stars look strange to me."

RING AROUND A STAR

JEFF SAT in the cockpit watching the stars that flew past their ship. All the windows were dark. No light could reach them. Only the fast neutrinos could paint the gray dots of stars in the mirrors. And the dots all looked alike.

"Well?" Ty gripped his arm. "How do we find Topaz?"

"Let's try Buzz," Jeff said. "He's had X-space experience. He was put on the team because his mastermind knows so much."

"Try him," Ty said. "I can watch the scope."

Jeff climbed down the ladder into the main cabin. It was a tall, round room, filled with their life-support equipment. Buzz's thick brown cocoon lay on a shock seat. Lupe stood by, whistling at it.

"We are lost," Jeff told her. "We need Buzz to help us locate Topaz."

She shook her head. "He's in his cocoon."

"What's wrong with him?"

"He's cut off," she said. "Something about X-space flight cuts his link to that other mind. He's all alone and he feels afraid. The same thing happened to him on our flight from his world to Earth." She tried to smile. "He will be all right when we get to Topaz."

"We may never get there unless he can help us now," Jeff said. "Will you ask him to try?"

"It's no use."

When Jeff insisted, she hummed over the cocoon. Nothing happened at first, but finally Buzz's head pushed slowly out. His dark eyes blinked blankly at Jeff.

"It's no good," Lupe said. "He just can't reach his sister-brothers."

"We've got to do something. Now." Jeff held on to the ladder with damp hands. "Lupe, you are a starman. You came to Earth with Buzz. Could — could you help pilot us to Topaz?"

Slowly, she shook her head.

"I learned how to travel in space from Buzz's brother-sisters," she said. "Their system is different from yours. Most of your instruments look strange to me. But you and Ty know this ship. With all those instruments and charts, can't the two of you locate Topaz?"

"Flight instruments aren't much use in X-space," he told her. "I guess you know compasses don't work here, because we are cut off from everything. The clock does help us guess how far we've gone, but nothing tells which direction."

"You do have star charts?"

He nodded. "But we can't make them fit any stars that we can see. The stars in the scope have no color. They're just gray dots. When you see them from a new direction, they're hard to recognize. Ty says they look like snowflakes in the wind."

"But you can see where they are," she said. "Even in the scope. You can figure distance and direction, from one star to the next. With those figures, you can pick them out on the charts."

"We tried," Jeff said. "But our charts cover just the main space lanes. We do have a lot of distance and position figures stored in our machine, but we are moving too fast to use them. The stars are gone before we get anything printed out."

"Maybe — " She hesitated, looking down at the brown cocoon. "Do you mind if I just take a look?"

"Please do," he said.

"Of course I don't have any charts. But Buzz's brother-sisters did help me learn a lot of distance and position figures."

"You don't mean you've remembered whole books of figures?"

"That multiple mind was my teacher," she said. "It taught me new ways to learn."

"Okay," he said. "Go to it."

Without a word, she followed him up the ladder. Ty gave her his seat in front of the scope.

Lupe sat watching the neutrino scope. Her dark eyes were opened very wide. A tiny furrow creased her forehead.

The mirrors showed three faint stars, gathered together. They dived out of nowhere, darted close to the ship, and vanished in the white mist behind. Three long minutes passed. Those three minutes, Jeff figured, had carried them another three light-years from where they ought to be.

"I know that star!" Relief smoothed the tiny wrinkle from Lupe's forehead. "I've figured its location with respect to the stars around it and checked the results against the tables I learned. That's the star you call Aldebaran."

For a moment nobody said anything. Lupe was pointing to one gray point near the edge of the forward mirror. Jeff leaned over to look at it, and suddenly caught his breath.

"Ty, she's right!" he whispered. "See that faint star by it? Aldebaran has a dim companion. It does look different by neutrinos, but now I recognize it."

He grinned gratefully at Lupe. Maybe the machine that picked her for the flight had no screws loose, after all.

Lupe began pointing out other objects on the mirrors. Aldebaran was drifting slowly across the bright lines on the side mirrors now, but she pointed at a little cloud of gray dots still on the forward mirror.

"See that group?" she said. "That's the swarm of stars you call the Hyades."

"If you say so, Lupe." Ty nodded, grinning weakly. "They still look like drifting flakes of snow to me. I will have to take your word."

Jeff had begun to feel at home in X-space. After all, he thought, this was really the same world he had always known. It just looked different because now he saw it in a different way, with fast neutrinos and not with light. He had learned the charts, back at school, and now he began to recognize the stars faster than Lupe could name them.

He got back his sense of mass and force and motion. The stars and their ship were masses to him now. The motions the forces caused were suddenly as clear to him as the motion of his own fingers when he closed his hand.

The stars were no longer dull gray points flying out of that far gray mist. They were old friends.

When Jeff began pointing out the stars, Lupe slipped out of the seat in front of the scope.

"May I go back to Buzz?" she asked Ty. "He needs me."

"Go ahead." Ty gave her a grateful smile. "Now I see why you were picked to come with us."

He nodded for Jeff to take her place.

"You are the pilot, Jeff," he said. "Next stop, Topaz!"

Jeff slid happily into the seat. Topaz was still hidden in that cloud of far-off stars ahead, and the sun had faded long ago into the white glow behind. But he knew Aldebaran. He knew the Hyades. He knew where to look for the Pleiades beyond them. The way to Topaz had become plain.

Jeff reached for the controls to point the ship toward Topaz. The little ship felt as steady as the Earth.

Ty stayed for a while to study the scope and the charts. Then he went down the ladder to the cabin. Jeff was alone in the cockpit until Lupe came back with food for him.

"Buzz feels better now," she said. "And Ty's sleeping."

She sat with him in the cockpit while he ate and sipped hot coffee. He asked about what Buzz's sister-brothers had taught her, and he tried to imagine those far worlds of Opal where she had grown up.

She pointed out the Pleiades, when they crept into the forward mirror, and he told her how he had learned to know them as the Seven Sisters, when he was still a child. He showed her the direction of Topaz, which was still too far to see.

He didn't want to think about what they would have to do when they came to Topaz. He didn't say anything about it, but he must have grown too quiet.

"What's wrong, Jeff?" she said suddenly. "Aren't we safe now?"

"I guess we are safe enough here." He tried to look cheerful. "With you to help us find the way."

"But you've got something on your mind."

"The real danger begins when we come to Topaz." He spoke slowly. "In the first place, we've no station there. No beacon to show us a safe place to cut out of X-space flight."

"We do have the scope." She nodded at the mirrors.

"But it shows us only the cores of stars. The neutrinos don't shine from anything else. The mirrors can't show planets or falling stars or rock hoppers — whatever they look like. When we cut out, we cut out blind."

For a long time Lupe didn't move or speak. She sat watching a near, bright star crawling out of the forward mirror. Then, with her light fingers, she touched his hand.

"We will make it, Jeff," she said softly.

He was not convinced, but he kept thinking of her after she was gone. He remembered the cool touch of her fingers, and was glad they had talked. All the dangers of Topaz were still ahead, just as real as ever, but somehow she had made him feel better about them.

Ty came to take the controls, and Jeff went to the cabin for a rest. When he came back, the Pleiades were a dim gray spot on the rear mirror. He slipped into the pilot's seat and watched the gray dots creeping out of the pale neutrino glow on the forward mirror.

"There!" He caught Ty's arm and pointed to a faint gray speck. "That's Topaz."

Jeff turned the ship, and Topaz floated out of the mist of farther stars. It grew as he slowed the ship to meet it, until its bright gray glare washed everything else out of the forward mirror. But the cockpit windows remained dark, for they were still in X-space flight.

"I've been thinking about where to cut out," Ty said. "Every star has a lot of junk around it. I mean planets, dust, gas. The junk gets thicker, closer to the star. To be quite sure we don't hit anything, we ought to cut out a long way this side of Topaz."

Jeff shook his head. "But that's just half the picture."

"I know," Ty said. "If we cut out too soon, we will have too far to fly in common space to reach the planets. We will have to waste too much time in low-speed flight. Though we will be safe from dust at low speeds, we will run too much chance of hitting something bigger — junk too small for us to see in time to dodge it, but heavy enough to do some damage."

"A tough choice," Jeff said.

"We've got to balance the risks of stopping too soon against the risks of stopping too late." Ty frowned at that gray blaze in the forward mirror, making up his mind. He straightened suddenly. "We will cut out at a billion miles."

Looking more at ease now that his mind was made up, he turned to Jeff.

"Your brother came to Topaz from this same direction," he said. "He had the same set of facts to work from. Perhaps he made the same decision. With any luck, we ought to cut out within a reasonable distance of where he did."

"It's nearly time to cut out," he said a moment later. "Better warn Lupe."

Ty took his place, and Jeff scrambled down the ladder into the cabin. He found Buzz out of his cocoon, sitting in Lupe's lap, and sucking a tube of Ty's shaving cream.

Lupe smiled at Jeff's puzzled expression. "Buzz eats oils. But he doesn't like the wax that somebody packed for him. He says the shaving cream tastes much better."

"We are cutting out now," Jeff told them. "Better get set."

Buzz whined and held on to Lupe until they put him back in the brown cocoon. Lupe wanted to stand over him, but Jeff made her take her own shock seat. He buckled her in and climbed back to the cockpit.

"Okay!" Ty grinned at Jeff. Firmly, with no fuss, he pulled back the mass-reduction lever. The stars in the scope flickered and went out, as the ship became too slow to catch their neutrinos. For a few seconds, all Jeff could see was the dim glow of the instrument board. Then the light of Topaz exploded through the cockpit windows. Losing speed, the ship seemed to spin and drop.

"Look!" Excitement had turned Ty's voice to a deep whisper. "Look at Topaz!"

The sudden glare of the new star ahead hurt Jeff's eyes. He shaded them, and blinked, and then he forgot everything else. Staring at the star, he forgot to be afraid.

"Look at that ring!" Ty said. "A ring around the star!"

Topaz was a giant blue star. It looked about a fifth the size of the sun to Jeff, but he knew that it was still ten times as far away as he was used to seeing the sun. He thought it must be twice its size. It had no planets that he could see.

Instead, it had a ring — a wide doughnut of bright white light, glazing in this strange black sky that only Ben and his crew had ever seen before. Topaz hung in the dark hole in the doughnut.

"It's like Saturn," Jeff whispered. "Like the rings of our Saturn."

But Ty wasn't listening. He sat leaning over the controls. Watching them, watching the blue blaze of Topaz, he was fighting for the life of their starship. He pulled the mass-reduction lever back, farther, farther, all the way.

These were the moments of greatest danger. There was no beacon to guide them, no entrance zone swept out. They were flying into unknown space, too fast to avoid anything in the way.

Jeff remembered the energy laws he had learned at Space School. The energy — and the damage — in hitting another object changed with the square of the speed. Whether it was a bat hitting a ball, a car hitting a truck, or the ship hitting a rock, the laws still held.

Twice the speed meant four times the energy, four times the damage. A hundred times the speed meant ten thousand times the damage. One rock could smash their starship.

Jeff heard the sound of their ship's jet pumps, building up a screen of magnetic fields that would push away small objects at any normal speed.

Now the ship was down to half the speed of light, but that was still far too fast. Jeff watched a red needle on the board, crawling slowly back toward a point marked NORMAL MASS. When the needle reached that point, their speed would be normal, too. The magnetic screen would be useful then.

Numbers flashed in Jeff's mind, like danger signs. Half the speed of light was ninety-three thousand miles a second. They could cut that ten thousand times, to nine miles a second. Ten thousand times ten thousand was a hundred million. By braking the ship to nine miles a second, they could cut the damage a hundred million times.

"Ten seconds . . ." Jeff started counting under his breath, measuring the time that red needle would take to reach NORMAL MASS. "Eight . . ."

"Jeff?" He jumped when Lupe spoke. "So that's Topaz!"

She had left her shock seat and climbed to the cockpit. She was staring through the windows at the star with the bright ring around it.

"Better get down," he whispered. "We aren't safe yet."

"Oh! I thought — "

She dropped down the ladder.

"Three . . ." Jeff looked back at the crawling needle. "Two . . ."

Slam!

At first he thought the motors had fired wrong again. But the old motors could not have made the hot red flash that surprised him, or the sharp blast that left a ringing in his ears. Air was roaring, when he could hear again. He blinked and found a hole torn in the hull just over Ty's head.

Their air was howling out into empty space.

"We've been hit!" The thought struck him like a blow.

But he knew what to do. He grabbed the orange-

painted sealing gun off the wall beside his seat, aimed at the black hole, and fired. A fat black balloon of sealing foam popped out and flew into the hole.

"Oh-oh!" His lips moved stiffly. "Hole's too big — "

But the foam ball caught on the torn metal edges. Air pressure squeezed it wider. In a second the roaring stopped. The hole was sealed.

Glad of air to breathe, Jeff looked again at the red needle. It had come to NORMAL MASS. The screen would shield them now.

"You did it!" Leaning back in his seat, he turned to Ty. "We are safe — "

His voice stuck when he saw Ty's face. The grin was frozen on it, under a red smear. Half of Ty's face was covered with blood.

"I guess we've finished the X-space flight." Ty's voice was very soft. "But you are the pilot now, Jeff. I can't see."

"BEN STONE CALLING . . ."

JEFF set the starship on auto pilot and reached under his seat for a medical aid kit.

"Let's get a bandage on you," he said to Ty. "Then we can help you down to the cabin — "

"That can wait," Ty broke in softly, "until we know what the score is."

"We are back to normal mass," Jeff said. "We can trust the screen while we take care of you."

He opened the medical kit.

"What hit us?" Lupe's dark head came up through the ladder well. "Buzz is all right again," she said. "He's back in touch with his sister-brother at the base on the moon, and the admiral wants to know what's — "

When she saw Ty's head, her eyes went blank.

"Oh! I didn't know." Her hands turned white, gripping the ladder. "Does it hurt much, Ty?"

"It hurts." Ty tried to grin.

"Buzz can help you." Her anxious eyes came to Jeff. "Let's get him down to the cabin, where Buzz will have room to work."

Jeff looked hard at her. "Is Buzz a doctor?"

"He's part of that multiple being," she said. "Its mind can see through his eyes and move his hands. It knows everything that all of his sister-brothers have learned. That makes Buzz better than most doctors."

Jeff shook his head. "We can't take a chance. Not with Ty's eyes."

"It's the best chance we have," Ty broke in. "Help me down the ladder."

Jeff guided his hands to the ladder. Down in the cabin, they helped him into a shock seat and buckled the straps. His face was gray under the dried blood.

Buzz was out of the brown cocoon. His saucer eyes and his fine fur shone softly gold again. His quick little hands with their three fingers took the medical kit from Jeff.

He bent over Ty. Suddenly he leaned closer, his golden eyes shining on the wound like two flashlights. His shrill whine startled Jeff.

"Ty is badly hurt," Lupe said. "Buzz says what hit him was a laser bolt."

"A signal, you mean?"

Buzz whistled again, not quite so sharply.

"Lasers are bundles of light waves, all alike and all in step," Lupe said. "This bolt had millions of times

too much power for just a signal. It exploded that hole in the hull. A bit of flying metal hit Ty in the face, but it was the bolt of light that burned his eyes."

"I saw a red flash." Jeff stared at Buzz. "And Ben's last message said that he was under laser attack. What I don't understand is how they could hit us so soon."

"When we cut out — " Ty's whisper was faint and broken with pain. "Coming back through the light — the ship caused a light burst. Something like a — sound boom. Rock hoppers — must have — seen the burst."

"So they were waiting for us," Jeff said. "Somewhere close. They hit us in the first minute. Long before our light burst had time to reach the ring or the star."

"Something out there — doesn't like us." Ty drew a sharp breath, and Jeff heard his teeth set against the pain. "Guess they'll hit us again — when they see us move."

"We will get to that," Jeff told him. "Just now we are taking care of you."

"Get Buzz to call the admiral," Ty whispered hoarsely. "Tell him — tell him how the hoppers shot at us. They didn't warn. There was no excuse. Ask him what he thinks — about his peace policy — now!"

"We are already reporting to the admiral," Lupe said. "He isn't giving any special orders. He says he's leaving it up to us. But his policy still stands. He wants us to find the hoppers and make peace with them."

"Trouble is — " Ty's whisper died, then came weakly back. "Trouble is — they found us first." He lay still.

Buzz bent over him, whistling at Lupe.

"Buzz isn't sure what he can do," she said. "But it's going to hurt, when he explores the wound. Buzz says we ought to give him something to put him to sleep, but there's nothing in the aid kit."

"I can stand some pain," Ty whispered.

"Wait!" Jeff broke in. "Can't we use a deep-sleep shot?"

Buzz whistled at Lupe.

"Buzz has heard about deep sleep," she said. "He wants to know more about it."

"It was invented to help men live through accidents in space," Jeff said. "It slows life to the very point of death. In deep sleep, you need no food or warmth or even air. You can wake up from it, if you get care in time."

Buzz whistled quickly, and Lupe said, "He wants to see the drug."

Jeff showed Buzz a sealed green package in the medical kit, then broke the seal to pull out a small needle and a timer.

"The needle is marked in hours," Jeff told him. "You set the slide for the weight of the patient. The smallest shot gives about three hours of deep sleep. The whole needle gives a thousand hours. That's the limit. The timer tells when care has to be started."

Buzz chirped.

"He thinks it ought to work," Lupe said. "If Ty's willing to try it."

Ty was fumbling weakly at the straps, trying to sit up in the shock seat. He spoke too loudly, his face toward the wall.

"Jeff?"

"Yes, Ty."

"Ask Buzz to go ahead." He stopped, and Jeff saw sweat on his face. "Jeff?"

"Right here, Ty."

"You are in command till I wake up."

Ty sank weakly back. His hand reached up and found Jeff's shoulder. He hung on, his fingers cold, while they waited.

Buzz was humming fast at Lupe. They sprayed their hands to clean them. They sprayed the wound. Buzz gave Ty a careful shot of the deep-sleep drug. Ty's hand grew tight on Jeff's shoulder, trembled, and suddenly eased.

Jeff watched as Buzz began the operation. His fur and eyes had turned bright blue again. His tiny hands seemed very quick and sure. He used the instruments from the kit as if he knew all about them.

Lupe was his helper. She looked pale and weak at first. Once she dropped a pink ball of cotton. But Buzz kept purring at her, asking for what he needed next. Soon she was working calmly, too busy to think of anything else.

When he saw that he was no longer needed, Jeff climbed back to the cockpit. If he was going to carry on the rescue mission, as commander of the ship, he had problems of his own to solve.

What were those "queer kinds of life" that Ben had found here? Where did they live, if Topaz had no planets? Why had he named them rock hoppers? How had they come to attack him?

Was the admiral wrong, Jeff wondered, to send Lupe and Buzz to search for peace? Shouldn't Earth be sending fighting ships through X-space instead, to crush the hoppers before they could carry space war to Earth?

The ship was still on auto pilot, gliding at low power toward Topaz. The pumps of the screen still drummed softly, like the beat of a great slow heart — but he knew the screen wouldn't stop laser bolts.

He wondered how far that first shot had come. Earth, he knew, had no laser weapon that could fire a shot even a thousand miles before it spread wider than the hole in the hull. Earth had no weapon of any kind that could hit such a small object as the ship in the first minute of fire.

Did that mean the hoppers were less than a thousand miles away? Or did it mean that the hoppers' weapons were far ahead of Admiral Serov's, in range and power?

With Ty in deep sleep, the answers to all those questions were up to Jeff.

He slipped into the pilot's seat and reached up to test the seal in the hull. The thick black sealing foam was already hard. He found no leak. But the next shot, he thought, might punch a larger hole.

When he looked outside, the view took his breath again. Half the sky was dusty black. The rest was filled with Topaz and its ring. The giant blue sun with its wide belt of white looked beautiful to him. Yet he knew there was danger in that strange sky.

The ship's screen showed nothing near. But there hadn't been time for that deadly bolt to come all the way from the ring.

Something was waiting out there, closer.

A dull, cold feeling sank into Jeff. He saw no way to find the lost ship. Not even if it were still whole. Not even if the rock hoppers would let him look for it.

In all the unknown space around Topaz, Ben's ship was less than a grain of dust. Jeff's naked eyes could see anything its size, perhaps a hundred miles away. The laser screen could find the lost ship at ten thousand miles.

But ten thousand miles was nothing here. The nearest edge of that strange ring was still tens of millions of miles away.

The figures mocked him. Even one million miles was a thousand thousand miles. A billion miles was a thousand million. When he tried to grasp those figures, and the distances they stood for, he felt like a tiny insect trapped in some great web.

He was still trying to think of a plan, when Lupe

came up the ladder behind him. Her face showed the strain, but her eyes remained bright.

"We have finished," she told him. "Ty was worse than Buzz first thought. The damage went behind his eyes, to the nerves. Buzz gave him another deep-sleep shot, to last until the tissues heal. We set the timer at a hundred hours."

"Will he — see?"

"Buzz isn't sure." Her voice was slow with trouble. "He hopes the eye nerves will heal, but he has never done this operation on a human being. We won't really know until we can wake Ty and take the bandage off."

"We need him now."

"I know we do," Lupe said. "We've been reporting to the admiral on the moon. Buzz says he's worried about us. He isn't giving any orders, because he isn't on the spot, but he wants to know everything that happens. He has some questions for you."

"All right," Jeff said.

Lupe whistled, and Buzz ran up the ladder. Lively as a monkey now, he chattered to her, hopped into the empty seat beside Jeff, and sat there looking out at Topaz. In the blue glare of the star, his big eyes turned bright green.

"The admiral wants your description of Topaz," Lupe said.

"It's twice the size of our sun." Jeff tried to put his facts in the exact way that the admiral would approve. "We've found no planets. The stuff that might have formed planets is still scattered all around the star, in a flat ring like the rings of Saturn.

"Really," he added, "the ring is three rings. We can see two dim circles that almost separate it. If it had formed planets, I think there would have been three of them.

"The ring system extends about a billion miles from Topaz," he went on. "That makes it somewhat smaller than our sun system. We cut out of X-space above the plane of the ring. We are moving now about sixty million miles from the outside edge of the ring."

"The admiral wants to know what the ring is made of."

"Dust, I guess," Jeff said. "Or maybe crystals of ice. It is stuff that never collected into planets. At this distance the screen doesn't show any individual parts."

"He wants to know if we've found any possible place for life to exist."

"None except the ring itself," Jeff said. "If life did begin in a ring, instead of on a planet, I don't know what it would be like. My brother's message mentioned rock hoppers. I don't know what they are."

Buzz whistled.

"The admiral has received your report," Lupe said. "Now he wants to know your plan of action."

Frowning, Jeff took another thirty seconds to finish making up his mind.

"We are going to place the X-space station at once,"

he said. "That will make the ship lighter. It will save fuel and give us more freedom of action. I hope that Ben and his men will see the station beacon and signal us. I see no better way to begin the search for them."

Buzz chirped sharply.

"The admiral has your reply," Lupe said. "He suggests that the beings of Topaz are likely to consider the dropping of the beacon as an enemy action. He suggests that you may draw their fire."

"I think we have to accept that risk," Jeff replied. "We still have a long flight through common space to reach the ring. Loaded with the station, we would be a sitting duck for any attack. If we let the station loose with the beacon dead, so far out here, we would never find it again."

Buzz made a sound like a trapped fly.

"The admiral has no advice for you," Lupe said. "He repeats that you are in full command. He wants us to keep him fully informed."

Buzz gave another whistle.

"Buzz doesn't think much of your plan," Lupe said. "But even his multiple mind can't suggest a better one."

"So we will try this," Jeff said. "We will drop the station and run. The hoppers may shoot at it. If they do, we may have a minute or so before their bolts get here. Try to see anything you can."

He turned a key on the instrument board and

punched a button to drop the station. The sharp nose cone spun away from their ship. Inside the cone, power flowed and machines came to life. Outside, a web spread to sweep objects from the entrance zone.

On the side of the station toward the far-off Earth, the neutrino beacon began flashing its signal through X-space, ready to guide new ships from Earth to Topaz — if any other ships ever came.

On the side toward Topaz, the laser beacon began winking orange and green, orange and green. Its winks could reach the nearest edge of the ring around the star. Jeff hoped they would reach Ben. He knew they would reach the waiting hopper.

"One . . ." Under his breath, he counted the seconds. "Two . . . three . . ."

He had opened the motor to full power and pushed the mass-reduction lever. Freed from all the tons of the station, the starship seemed light as a bird. They darted away from the wink of the beacon.

"Five . . . six . . . seven . . ."

He was counting to get the distance of the hopper. The light of the beacon would take time to reach it. Its laser bolt would take time to come back. Each second meant nearly a hundred thousand miles.

"Eleven . . . twelve . . . thirteen . . ."

Behind their ship, the beacon blinked red once, instead of green. A small ball of bright yellow fire ballooned in black space. It turned pale and went out. The beacon did not wink again.

Though Jeff had expected this, he felt a shock. The station had been an open gate on the long road back to Earth. Now it was closed. They couldn't go back.

"A flash! I saw a red flash." Lupe was pointing. "There — just above the ring of Topaz."

Jeff nodded. "That was the laser. That's where the hopper is. I think about a million miles from here."

Buzz was purring softly.

"He thinks we should head that way," Lupe said. "He must find the hoppers, to make peace with them."

"I don't think they mean to give us much time for talking peace," Jeff said, but he turned the ship toward that spot in the dark sky above the ring.

The starship flew fast. They had covered half of that million miles when the screen picked up another laser beam. Buzz's bright blue fur turned pale.

"This is not another attack," Jeff told him. "It's too weak to harm anything."

Unlike the deadly spears of red light that had blinded Ty and wrecked the station, this was the very thinnest thread of light, as fine as the ray of a far-off star.

"A signal!" Jeff whispered. "A voice!"

He bent over the screen, working to increase the signal and shut out the noise. At last a hoarse, hollow voice boomed in the cockpit, still mixed with the hiss and crash of noise.

"Starman Ben Stone calling . . ."

RAINBOW OF ROCKS

THE HOARSE VOICE was cut off sharply, as if the thin thread of light had broken. Odd noises drummed and howled in the cockpit.

"Ben!" Jeff looked up at Lupe. "He's still alive."

Quickly, he bent over the screen. His fingers worked furiously to mend the thread of light. Nothing but noise. But at last the voice came out again.

"Starman Ben Stone, calling anybody. Our ship has been under laser attack. We've lost air and power. Now we are in the rocks around Topaz, caught in a rock hopper's web . . ."

Roaring noise drowned the voice.

Jeff searched for it again, but all he got was the crash and hiss and scream of noise. At last he gave up.

"What does it mean?" Lupe whispered. "What's a rock hopper's web?"

"I don't know what it is." Staring at the shining ring of Topaz, Jeff felt a cold prickling at the back of his neck. "Anyhow," he said, "we know where it is. We can chart it on the screen. Ben's voice came from the outside edge of that ring — from a point sixty million miles ahead of us. The question — "

He stopped to look at Lupe.

"The question now is, do we answer?"

"Why not?" Lupe asked. "If your brother is asking for help."

"Whoever fired at us is probably waiting just ahead," Jeff said. "If we use power enough to reach sixty million miles, he's sure to see our signal beam. I think he will shoot — "

Buzz chattered suddenly, shrinking away from Jeff.

"His body is frightened." Lupe was standing just behind his seat, and she bent to stroke his shining fur. "But his multiple mind says we must answer. His mind says we can't make peace by hiding."

"I don't see how we can make peace by letting them shoot at us," Jeff said. "But still I think we must answer. I want to let Ben know we are here."

Buzz tugged at Lupe until she sat down in the seat with him. He scrambled into her lap and sat blinking up at her. His fur was turning dark.

"Starship Topaz B, to Topaz A." Jeff's eyes were on the clock on the instrument board, watching the second hand. "Ben, we are on the way—"

Smash!

Something exploded. A red flash blinded him for a moment, so that he couldn't read the clock. There was the smell of burned paint in the cockpit, and he heard Buzz whining.

"Did they hurt us?" Lupe whispered.

"Don't know yet."

Jeff listened for leaking air. When he could see, he blinked to read the instrument board. Air pressure normal. Fuel pressure normal. Power normal. Mass reduction normal. Everything seemed normal, until he noticed that the sound of the pumps had stopped.

"They got the screen," he said. "But we can go on without it — as long as we are lucky."

"Will they shoot again?"

"Wish I knew." He glanced at the clock. "They hit us something like six seconds after our beam went on. That would mean they're still about half a million miles ahead."

"What do we do now?"

"Ben's out beyond them," Jeff said. "We've got to keep going."

Buzz twittered in Lupe's lap. He was clinging fast to her, both thin arms wrapped around her neck. His eyes were bright green, peering at Jeff.

"If you are afraid, so am I." Jeff tried to grin at him. "I think there is good reason to be afraid. Earth has no weapon that could hit a moving starship half a million miles away — or even a tenth that far."

He looked up at Lupe.

"If the hoppers get into X-space — if they break through Sun Point — all our planets will be at their mercy. They can stay out of range while they cut us to pieces."

Buzz chirped weakly.

"He says we must go on," Lupe said, "because we must make peace."

They went on. Jeff pushed the mass-reduction lever as far as he dared, changing mass to speed, hoping to make them harder to hit. Watching the clock, watching the screen, he waited for another shot.

"Here we are!" He looked at Buzz. "If you want to make peace, we've come to the point where they fired at us."

Searching the space around them, Jeff saw nothing except dusty darkness and the rings of Topaz. The screen showed nothing.

Lupe lowered her voice. "Where are they now?"

"Hard to say." Jeff frowned. "We can't see far enough. They've got plenty of room to hide, until they want to shoot again."

"What now?"

"We will go on," Jeff said. "We will look for Ben's ship in that rock hopper's web."

Buzz moved around in Lupe's lap. Humming softly as she held Buzz close, she looked up with a quick smile for Jeff. He pushed the mass-reduction lever farther over.

"If we get hit, we get hit." He grinned back at her. "With our screen dead, we are just as safe at twice the speed."

That was not exactly true. At twice the speed they would hit meteors twice as fast, and each one they hit would do four times the damage. Lupe knew it and so did Jeff, but neither said anything.

They flew on toward the clean bright edge of that far ring. Lupe and Buzz were busy reporting to the admiral. Lupe questioned Jeff. She read the ship's log to Buzz. She figured out pen scratches from the recording instruments. Sometimes she spoke English to Buzz, and sometimes she talked his own language. They went all over the ship, observing the rings of Topaz through the cockpit windows, studying the instrument board, scrambling down the ladder to examine Ty, climbing farther down to inspect the mass-reduction gear.

"I'm afraid all this won't help us find your brother." Lupe gave Jeff a look of sympathy. "But it's what the admiral wants. What we've learned won't be wasted."

Jeff said he understood. He tried to feel as cool and brave as Lupe seemed. He even pushed the speed of the ship a little higher, but he had to pull it back when he began to hear the dust.

The dust was a whisper at first, a hiss of small hits against many thousand bits of matter too small for the auto pilot to steer around. The whisper changed to a rattle of hail when they hit too many grains of dust too fast.

Their speed made each grain a small bomb that exploded against the thick shield over the cockpit. In the deadly seconds of cut out, when they were still near the speed of light, one small speck of matter could have smashed the ship. Even now, though their lower speed had cut the force each time dust exploded, they were in danger.

The admiral wanted another report.

"The dust seems to lie in clouds," Jeff said. "The closer we get to Topaz and the ring, the thicker the clouds get. Flying through them, we have to balance two different risks. If we fly too fast, some larger grain of dust may crack the shield. But we are still too far from the ring. If we fly too slow, we may be too late to do anything for Ben and his crew."

"The admiral has your message," Lupe repeated after Buzz's chirp.

They pushed on toward the ring.

Once Lupe took the controls to let Jeff rest while they flew between the clouds, but another storm of dust brought Jeff back to the cockpit. With every hiss and crash, his nerves tightened. The sky seemed to him like a dreadful pit. Sometimes he had a dizzy feeling that the ship was falling all the way to the hot blue heart of Topaz.

Buzz came to join Lupe in the cockpit, carrying a tube of toothpaste. He waved it eagerly at Jeff, his bright blue face wrinkled into a grin.

"He got it out of your space bag," Lupe said. "He wants your permission to eat it."

"Help yourself, Buzz." Jeff tried not to laugh at him. "I'm glad you like it."

Buzz climbed into Lupe's lap, sucking at the tube. He squeezed it flat, carefully licked the smears from his lips and his slim hands, and then purred softly at Jeff.

"He thanks you very much," Lupe said. "It was delicious."

He was soon asleep in her lap.

"His mind is as old as his people." She smiled down at him. "Even his body is older than I am. He hasn't grown an inch in all the time I've known him. But time is different for him and his people. In some ways he's still a baby."

Jeff leaned forward to check the screen. It showed nothing nearer than the bright ring of Topaz. When he tested the laser, all he got was a new burst of noise that made Buzz cry in his sleep.

Quickly he snapped it off again. They were flying between two clouds, where there was no roar of dust. It felt good to have a little time of quiet, with Lupe beside him. He talked to her about his life-long attempt to keep up with Ben.

"Sometimes I'm afraid that I care more about myself than I do about rescuing Ben," he told her.

Lupe sat silent for a time, watching the ring of Topaz and stroking Buzz's bright fur.

"Self does matter," she said. "But I guess I have another sort of self. Or maybe I should say I never had a self."

The dust was whispering again. Jeff pulled back the mass-reduction lever and waited for her to go on.

"You see, I grew up where nobody had a self. Not like Earth people do. Buzz was my little brother-sister. Our larger sister-brothers nursed us and taught us and made us behave. But they all belonged to that one great self."

She looked sharply at Jeff to see if he understood.

He wasn't quite sure he did, but he nodded and waited for her to make it clear.

"Buzz has a self sometimes," she said. "Just because he's so very young. But when the self hurts, he can always go back to his cocoon. The self sleeps, when he's in the cocoon. It makes him part of that great mind."

"I see." Jeff nodded slowly. "Or at least I think I do."

"I always wanted to be like them, too," Lupe said. "But I had no cocoon — I nearly died once, when I crawled into Buzz's cocoon and couldn't get out. But I always knew I wasn't like Buzz and his people."

Her voice had turned solemn.

"I wasn't made like them. I couldn't think like them. I couldn't share their common mind. I couldn't learn to be the way they are, each one living for the great common self to which they all belong."

She sat silent for a time, biting her lip.

"Yet I wasn't human, either." Her troubled eyes came back to Jeff. "My parents were gone before I can remember. There were no other Earth people on the planet. I didn't see a human being until I was twelve years old. I didn't know what a human being was."

She sat up straight and tried to smile.

"Of course it has been great fun, traveling to Earth and knowing people and going to school. Earth is nearly as wonderful as the worlds of Opal." She shook her head, looking down at Buzz again. "But still sometimes I don't know who or what I am."

"I think you don't have enough feeling of self," Jeff said. "You learned to do everything for your sister-brothers, and nothing for yourself."

He looked out at Topaz, thinking.

"Maybe I'm too much the other way," he said at last. "Maybe that's why I'm always trying to catch up with Ben — because I have to prove myself. I wish I were more like you."

"I didn't mean that," Lupe said quickly. "I like you fine the way you are."

That was all he heard, because he had seen a red flicker in the screen. Quickly, he bent to pick up the signal. Noise boomed in the cockpit. Ben's voice came out of the speaker like a shower of gravel.

" — calling anybody. . . . We've lost air and power. Now we are in the rocks around Topaz, caught in a rock hopper's web — "

The signal faded out.

Jeff searched again for the thread of light that carried it, but all he found was thunder. He snapped the speaker off and looked at Lupe.

"Ben doesn't know we are here," he said. "That wasn't an answer to our call. It was the same distress message, repeated. I think we will have to call Ben again."

"If we do, won't the hoppers shoot?"

"I don't know." He peered out into the darkness. "We've come fifty million miles beyond where they were —"

Buzz woke up in Lupe's lap. He blinked his green eyes at Topaz, and whined at Lupe.

"He thinks the hoppers followed us," she said. "He thinks they'll shoot. But he thinks we ought to call anyway."

"Why are the hoppers after us?"

Buzz chirped at Lupe.

"He doesn't know," she said. "He doesn't understand them. But he says we have to call."

"Get ready," Jeff warned. "I don't know what will happen. And report this to the admiral."

Buzz squeaked the message.

Jeff spoke slowly and clearly into the speaker. "Ben, this is Jeff —"

He never finished. Something exploded and rocked the ship. A red blaze flashed through the cockpit. For a while Jeff was deaf and blind. Before he could see, his ringing ears began to pick out sounds.

The dying sound, like a toy running down, was Buzz. The rising sigh, changing to a wild scream, was air leaking out of the ship. The slam was the door, sealing off the rear part of the starship.

"They are close," Jeff whispered. "They hit us hard."

"Are you hurt, Jeff?" Lupe asked.

"I can't see yet," he said. "Everything's green. Is Buzz all right?"

"Yes," Lupe answered. "He went back in his cocoon."

Jeff wiped the tears out of his eyes. Shapes were coming back into the green. He blinked at the instrument board.

"We got hit twice," he said at last. "One bolt knocked out the sending set, so we can't call Ben again. The other hit the rear of the ship and killed our power." He tried to see Lupe, but she was only a pale green shape. "We are drifting now, out of control."

The green shape made a frightened gasp.

"What can we do?"

"You can watch the instruments and keep the admiral posted," he said. "But first check to see about Ty. I will try to get the power on. That safety door sealed off the rear of the ship. I can go out in a space suit."

He squeezed her hand and scrambled quickly down the ladder.

Everything was still a dim green, but Jeff felt his way into the forward air lock. His training had made him at home in it, so he didn't need to see. He squeezed into the jet suit, sealed the helmet, and pulled the ring that would push him out of the ship. The lock moved and shot him into space.

For a second he thought he was really blind, because all he saw was darkness. Then he found the gleam of his safety line and followed it.

Jeff turned his head and found the star Topaz. Huge and blue, it hurt his aching eyes. Its ring was a terrible rainbow of white fire curving across the dusty dark.

His old fear caught him for a moment, when he saw Topaz. But now he had no time for fear.

He turned his eyes away. Twisting in space like a falling cat, he found the ship, floating close behind him.

The suit was powered like a small ship with its own jets, but he didn't need them now. A tug at the safety line sent him floating back to the starship. He found a long, ugly cut punched into the rear of their ship.

The hole was too big for his sealing gun. He had to go back to the lock for a repair pod. Working fast, he sprayed the skin of the ship around the long wound, and rolled out a thick sealing strip over it like a bandage.

When the strip had set, he went into the ship through the rear lock to test the seal. It held. With air pressure back to normal, he climbed out of the suit and went to work on the power cables.

It took a long time to put them all together again. At last the dead ship came back to life. Lights came on. The safety door opened itself. He climbed back through the cabin to the cockpit.

Lupe jumped when he touched her. "Is Ty okay?" he asked.

"I don't know," she said. "He never moves or anything. He's so still that he frightens me."

"That's the deep sleep," Jeff assured her. "He will be all right unless something hits him."

Jeff had a moment of panic when he glanced at the instrument board. The repairs had taken too long. They were too close to the ring of Topaz, flying far too fast.

He dived past Lupe into the pilot's seat and hauled back the mass-reduction lever, changing speed to normal mass. Firing all jets at full thrust, he fought to slow the starship.

Dust hissed and thundered against the shield. He tried to steer around the thickest clouds, and the roaring died back to a whisper as the ship slowed. The ring loomed near.

"We are slamming into the rainbow," he shouted to Lupe. "Better have Buzz tell the admiral what it is. It isn't dust or ice. It's rocks. Dry, broken rocks!"

THE ROCK HOPPER'S WEB

THE SCREEN flickered red.

Fighting to stop the ship, Jeff didn't see it until Lupe caught his arm and pointed. Then he picked up the signal. Ben's voice rang loud and clear.

" — lost air and power. Now we are in the rocks around Topaz, caught in a rock hopper's web — "

The signal was cut off sharply, but Jeff had already marked its source on the charts. He swung the ship toward it.

"That's the same call." He turned to Lupe, with a worried frown. "Ben still doesn't seem to know we are here."

Buzz had come up the ladder, whistling to Lupe. Buzz and Lupe were now constantly in touch with the admiral.

A loud sound suddenly killed the thrust that pushed the ship forward. They drifted dead in space, too near that wall of flying rocks. For a second Jeff thought they had hit some stray rock from the ring. He listened for the sound of leaking air, but all he heard was silence.

"The boosters." He peered at the instrument board. "Those boosters that the admiral said we would have to nurse along. They're gone. Let me see if I can fix them."

Jeff crawled along the ladder to the rear. "They're really gone," he said when he came back. "We've no parts or tools to repair them."

"We are a long way from any spare parts." Lupe tried hard to smile. "What now?"

"I see just one thing to try," Jeff said. "The ship's dead, but my jet suit still works. Maybe I can reach Ben in that — "

"And leave us here?"

"We can't just wait for the ship to crash into those rocks," he said. "If I can find Ben — if Ben and his men are still alive — maybe we can use his boosters. Maybe we can use parts from them to repair our ship."

"Be honest, Jeff!" she whispered. "Do we have a chance?"

"Not much of one," he said, "but we can't just quit."

She nodded slowly. "I guess you have to go. I — I will stay with Buzz and Ty."

"Watch the screen," he told her. "Keep in contact with the admiral. The way the ship is drifting, you ought to have about ten hours before you crash into those rocks. I will try to get back before that time. If I don't make it, you and Buzz had better take deep sleep."

He found an aid kit for her. She let him put it in her hand, without looking at it.

"And the hoppers?" she asked, her voice shaking. "If they attack — "

Jeff wanted to tell her they wouldn't attack. He wanted to say he would find them and make peace with them, the way the admiral wanted it. But he couldn't say anything. He left her in the cockpit, without looking back. He checked the jet suit and crawled inside. The lock shot him out of the ship.

He drifted outside, feeling lost and small. Half the sky was darkness. The other half was rocks, shining in the bright, cold light of Topaz.

The rocks all looked alike at first, except that some were large and some were small. They were all sharp. He was falling toward them, and fear swept through him like a freezing wind.

He shook his head in the space helmet, trying to get back his sense of mass and force and motion. Each rock, he knew, was moving around Topaz like a tiny planet — a planet with no air or water or any common kind of life. Each rock was a mass.

Thinking of it that way made Jeff feel better. Each rock was now itself. He knew where he was, and he had a good idea of the point in the rocks from which Ben had called. He threw off the safety line and made for that point.

The suit flew like a toy ship. Though it had no mass-reduction gear to multiply its speed, the rocks were near enough. The starship shrank to a silver spark that went out in the endless dark behind. The rocks grew larger, pouring out of space like an icy water-fall.

He searched them with the laser in his helmet, hoping for another call from Ben. He needed the signal to guide him toward the lost ship. No signal came.

He considered calling Ben. The sending machine was a thick black tube, like a heavy flashlight, snapped to the belt of his suit. Once he aimed it at the rocks and prepared to speak, but then he changed his mind.

Ben had never answered the other signals he had sent, and he didn't want the sort of answer the hoppers had been making. He snapped the tube back to his belt and flew on toward the blazing wall.

It was thinner than he had thought. The ring of Topaz was nearly two billion miles across, from rim to rim, but no more than ten miles thick. Now he could see through it, between the scattered swarms of broken stone, to scraps of black sky beyond.

He circled outside the whirling wall, near the rocks from which Ben had called. Or were these really the same rocks? He couldn't be sure, within a dozen miles. He had no way to know how deep in the ring Ben had been.

He searched the rocks for Ben, for the lost ship,

for any sort of web. He listened, and heard no signal. Shading his eyes from the hot glare of Topaz, he looked through the glasses built into his helmet. He saw only rocks, pouring around the big blue sun like broken ice in an endless shallow river.

Yet he knew he had to go on.

If the rock hopper's web wasn't in sight, it must be deeper in the rocks. Jeff dived into the strange river. Splintered rocks spun past him. Bits of rock filled the black sky behind him. The blue blaze of Topaz dimmed to a cold, blue gloom. Still he saw no starship.

He flew on, looking for a web, listening for Ben. He dodged flying chips the size of bullets and flying rocks the size of houses, until they grew thin in the dark space ahead. He had come all the way through the cloud, and still he hadn't found the lost ship.

Something hit the leg of his suit like an electric shock. Blue sparks showered around him. He tried to pull free from the thing against him, but it hung on.

He twisted the stiff suit and found a wire.

One bright strand, smaller than his little finger, stretched away to his right and left as far as he could see. Here and there, bits of rock stuck to it. They marked out a line through the cloud, even where he couldn't see the wire itself.

Shaken, he kicked at the wire. Bright sparks danced around his boot. A new shock hit his foot.

His boot stuck fast. Before he could think, he grabbed the wire with his right hand. He meant to push it off, but new sparks sprayed him. A sharper shock hit his arm. His armored glove stuck fast.

He gasped for breath and tried to understand. The wire was a trap. The electric current had made it stick to the metal of his suit. He was trapped like a fly in a spider's web —

A rock hopper's web! This was the web that had caught Ben's crippled starship. For that first moment, all Jeff could do was wonder what kind of creature would weave a metal web in a cloud of flying rocks and make electric shocks to kill its prey.

Trembling in the heavy suit, he twisted around to look back and forth along the wire. Far away, he saw a flying stone strike it and bounce. That puzzled him, even in his state of shock.

Why had the rock bounced, while he stuck fast? Why did some rocks stick? His eyes traced the wire to the nearest rock and saw a dull gleam of metal. So that was the answer!

Metal ores were fused by the current and stuck to the wire. Rocks that didn't contain metal bounced off. The web, he saw, was a kind of tool, useful to collect bits of rich ore out of the flying rocks, and it had collected him.

With all his strength, Jeff twisted against the shining wire. He tried to kick with his boot. He tried to open his frozen glove. All he did was hurt himself.

Hot sparks whirled around him. Heavy shocks struck and his body jumped with pain. He couldn't break free. The wire stuck to his leg and his boot and his glove.

When the shocks stopped at last, he hung from the wire limp and worn out. Gasping for breath, he felt damp with sweat and a little sick from the shocks.

He tried to decide what to do. One hand was still free. He had the suit itself, with its equipment. He still had more than half a tank to fuel his jets.

Maybe the jets could pull him free. At least they were something he could try. Using the padded controls inside the helmet, he didn't even need his hands to work them. He moved around so that the jet thrust would be straight away from the wire and pushed the chin button for full power.

The pale blue jets licked out around the wire, but nothing else happened. There wasn't even another shock. The push of the jets had been too weak, he thought, for the keeper of the web to notice it at all.

He searched for a better plan.

The tools he had used in his work on the starship were still clipped to the suit. With his free hand, he found a cutting tool. Holding it very carefully in his clumsy left hand, he tried to cut the web.

Sparks blazed around the tool. He felt it soften, saw hot metal splash. His glove slipped against the wire. He got it away before it stuck, but new shocks hit as if to punish him.

Every time his muscles jumped with the shocks, the laser machine thumped against his armored leg. That gave him a new idea. Though the little machine was not a weapon, its light had power.

It was a long time before he had the strength to move again. Then he reached for the machine. Gripping it under his pinned right arm, he twisted the knob from VOICE to CODE, because CODE used full power. He slid the range to the sharpest beam.

He got the machine back into his left hand, and pointed it very carefully at the bright wire on his right. With his thumb, he squeezed the code key. The instant blade of bright green light sliced the wire.

The cut wire contracted like a broken rubber band, dragging him into a cloud of rocks. Half blind and stiff with pain, he held to his plan. He bent his stuck leg, as he spun through the rocks. He moved his right arm to bring the whipping wire into reach. Then he cut at the web with his blade of light. Green fire flashed.

He was free!

The taste of blood was in his mouth, where he had bitten his lip. His body was cold and weak and quaking. For a long time, all he could do was fight for his breath.

When he could move again, he used the laser to slice bits of wire from the sole of his boot and the metal around his leg. He tried to cut the web from the grip of his steel glove, but only burned his hand. His right hand was still a useless fist.

He clipped the machine back to his belt and looked for the broken web. One end of the wire was lost somewhere in a dim swarm of rocks, but he found the other. A gleaming thread, with its rough beads of captured metal, it led away into the rocks.

He followed it.

Keeping a careful distance from it, he watched the rocks that touched the web and bounced or stuck. He watched behind him and ahead. He was looking for the keeper of the web, who he thought would come out to see what had happened.

Miles down the wire, he saw a knot. Something bright was wrapped in coils of wire. Gleaming strands stretched in four directions from it. When he came close enough, he could see that the captured thing was Ben's starship.

Ugly wounds had been cut in its bright skin. Some were patched and some were not. Looped many times around it, the coils held it fast. He saw no sign of life.

Ben had to be alive, because they had heard his voice. Jeff gripped the laser machine with his right arm. He twisted the knob back to VOICE and slid the range to NEAR. He pointed the machine at the trapped wreck —

"Starman Ben Stone, calling anybody."

The loud call rang in Jeff's helmet, before he could speak.

" — under laser attack." The voice was Ben's, the words were those he had heard before. " — in the rocks around Topaz, caught in a rock hopper's web — "

Ben's strained voice broke off, exactly where it always did, but Jeff had seen the dull red flicker of the signal. It wasn't in the captured ship. It was far off in the rocks, out along a strand of the web. How could that be?

Had Ben been forced to abandon his ship?

Jeff pointed the machine toward that dying flicker in the cloud. He was about to answer, to tell Ben he was here — but doubt checked him.

Too many times, his own calls had brought deadly fire. That was hard to understand, because he knew his brother's voice. He stopped to think. He had come a long way to earn this chance to rescue Ben, and he couldn't afford to throw it away.

A huge rock was sailing slowly past the web, too far away to touch the tangling wires. He steered the suit toward it. Floating behind it, he pointed the machine again into the rocks where he had seen that flicker.

"Ben!" he shouted into the machine. "It's Jeff — "

The flicker came back, far off in the gloomy blue. It grew brighter, terribly bright. He ducked behind the rock, just in time. Blinding red fire shattered chips off the rock.

Jeff drifted in his stiff suit behind the rock, holding the machine with his sore left hand. The bright flicker had given him one glimpse of the thing that had been calling him with Ben's voice and shooting at him.

It wasn't Ben. It was not a man. It was something dim and strange. Jeff couldn't see it clearly through the great cloud of blue rocks. But he knew it had to be the hopper.

THE KEEPER OF THE WEB

IT WAS A LONG MINUTE before Jeff could move. Then he swam to the other side of the shattered rock and looked out.

All he saw at first were broken rocks whirling through dim blue gloom. When he caught sight of the captured starship in the web, it was far behind him. The rock he was holding onto had already carried him past it.

Ahead of him, light shone on bright wire. His eyes followed that light, and he found the heart of the web. He stared at it in wonder. Many bright strands came together there, all beaded with sharp chunks of captured metal. Where they joined, they were woven into a kind of ball. The ball was covered with bits of dark ore and gray rock, so that it was hard to see. It looked hollow. Jeff thought it must be a kind of den. The keeper of the web, he thought, must live inside.

But the rock hopper was not there.

Jeff saw another dull flicker out in the cloud, far beyond that woven ball. Ben's hoarse voice was again in his helmet, carried to him on the shivering red light.

" — in the rocks around Topaz, caught in a rock hopper's web — "

The voice was Ben's, but now he knew that the call for help was just another trick. He didn't answer. Instead, he floated close behind the flying rock, his right fist anchored in a crack, waiting for the hopper.

In a few moments he saw it. It was coming home, climbing along a beaded wire toward the gray ball at the center of the web. It was big, and coming fast.

Nothing Jeff had ever seen was like it. Its five arms were thick and powerful where they joined its body, but thin as whips where they wrapped around the beaded wire. The arms were bright as silver, but the body was black — black, round, flat and with no head.

A dull red light winked at him suddenly from the top of its body. Ben's stolen voice rumbled like thunder in his helmet.

" — rocks around Topaz, caught — "

Jeff pulled himself farther back out of sight, but kept his eyes on the hopper. The red winking stopped. The creature climbed on again toward that dark ball. Although it was traveling fast, Jeff saw that it had a queer sort of limp.

Four of the arms whipped their quick thin tips around the beaded cable to pull it along, but the fifth

arm dragged behind like a broken snake. Jeff realized the hopper must have been hurt.

It came to the central ball and stopped there, outside a dark flat patch that he thought might be a sort of door. He watched it from his rock, waiting for his chance.

If it went on to mend its web where he had cut it, he might have time to slip down to Ben's ship. He might have time to see what had really happened to Ben and his starmen. With luck, if his power held out, he might be able to cut the ship free.

But the hopper didn't go on. It bent down suddenly, the fifth arm trailing limply. For a moment Jeff thought it was creeping into the den, perhaps to nurse its hurt arm.

Instead, it jumped at his rock.

Perhaps it had seen Jeff's head. Perhaps it had figured out where he had been when he answered its call. Jeff didn't wait to wonder. He picked another rock behind him and flew for it at the full thrust of his jets.

The sharp surface of the second rock shone red. He saw his own black shadow like a flat animal crawling on it. The hopper's light had cast the shadow, and it brought him Ben's booming voice.

He didn't look back. He shut his eyes and crossed his arms over the face plate of his helmet, waiting for the hopper to send out its beam.

When it came, it covered him with red fire. It burned his face in the helmet and hurt his shut eyes. It battered his suit like hail. Its full force struck the fuel tank and the power cell packed on his back. He felt the jets fire and quit.

When the hammering stopped, everything looked dim and green, but he could see that he was whirling toward the rock ahead, out of control. His jets were dead.

Yet Jeff had expected something worse. He had expected a bolt strong enough to kill him. Feeling lucky to be alive, he twisted his body to reach for a point of the rock as he sailed by. He caught it with his left hand and hung on. His stiff glove slipped and held. He pulled himself behind the rock.

The hopper was very close. Strangely, Jeff thought, it had a kind of beauty, too. Its coiled silver arms were bright and graceful, and the scales of its body were like black jewels.

Without the jets, he couldn't run. He had to fight. The admiral's policy of peace among the stars meant nothing to him now. Trying not to hurry, he turned the knob of his machine back to CODE and pushed the range as high as possible. Leaning carefully around the rock, he fired at the middle of the hopper's flat body.

The machine was not meant to be a weapon. He was not expecting to hurt the hopper much, but he saw dark puffs of smoke where his small darts of bright green light hit the shiny scales. He saw the silver arms knotting, twisting up to shield the body.

Jeff tried to duck back behind the rock. But his frozen right fist slipped when he tried to push against it. The red glare of the hopper's fire caught half his body.

Heat blazed through his suit, searing his body. He slipped the machine back under his right arm. Snatching wildly with his free left hand, he caught a corner of the rock and pulled himself to cover.

He hung there behind the rock until the pain went away, wondering why the bolt hadn't killed him. He couldn't believe that his own shots had really hurt the hopper. Perhaps its strange strength had been used up.

When he could move, Jeff looked up and saw that the hopper had reached his rock. Four thin silver coils were looped over the sharp points of the rock

to anchor the hopper. A quick bright tip reared up from the rock, searched back and forth, and whipped at Jeff.

Jeff fired wildly with the green blade of his sender. Dark smoke puffed from the bright coils. They moved back away from him.

The hopper's body must have crept around the rock behind him, while he fought its arms. The red glare of its laser struck him from behind. Jeff leaned against the rock and tried to shoot back, but the fire blinded him.

When he could see again, the body was near him on a flat face of the rock. All its limbs were gone. It was shaped like a round black cushion, three yards across and one yard tall. Five big yellow eyes were spaced around it, one just above the short gray stump of each missing arm. The hopper's arms were moving away through the rocks, swimming like silver snakes in an icy river.

Jeff saw a faint red glow in the middle of the black cushion. It was the laser. He knew now that it was no machine, but a living part of the hopper.

The hopper moved itself to point toward him. He tried to scramble out of the way of its red bolt, but his jets were dead and his battered body wouldn't move. All he could do was wait.

". . . lost air and power . . ."

The red glow faded, until Ben's captured voice was only a dying whisper in his helmet.

". . . caught . . ."

The hopper, Jeff realized, had used up all its power. This was his chance to kill it, to even the score for what it had done to Ben and Ty. He pointed the machine into the nearest yellow eye. Furiously, he thumbed the firing key.

The hopper's wide eye blinked, but nothing else happened. Jeff's machine had caught the full force of that last bolt from the hopper's laser. Now it was dead. He dropped it and looked back into that great yellow eye.

"Now what?" he muttered at the hopper, though he knew it couldn't hear him. "I'm not sure about the rules of the game. But I can't hurt you. I hope you can't hurt me."

His air smelled stale and the battered suit cramped his body. He couldn't think of anything to do. With the jets dead, he couldn't get away. With the laser dead, he couldn't fight.

All he could do was watch the hopper.

It glared back at him, but it couldn't move, with its silver arms gone. And now that its power was dead, it couldn't hurt him.

Jeff breathed his bad air. He twisted in the stiff metal of his suit. How had this queer kind of life been born, here in the ring of Topaz? Life on Earth had come out of the warm and friendly sea. Life would have to be different, he thought, to live in this cloud of cruel rocks with no air. It would have to be as marvelous, he thought, in its own strange way, as the living things of Earth.

He wondered if the hopper was really metal, or partly metal, as it looked. Was the life of the rocks based on metal, the way the life of Earth was based on water? Did it eat the scraps of metal collected in its web? Was that its source of energy? Was that deadly web spun out of its own metal body, as a spider spins its web?

He wondered how the hopper was made, to let it come apart. For he knew that his own weak fire had not cut off its silver arms. They had simply turned loose and flown away, like separate beings. No wounds were left where they had been, just smooth gray stumps.

He wondered why the creature had come to meet him alone. He thought it must have mates, perhaps by the million. Certainly the attack on his own starship, out beyond the ring, must have been begun by other beings, because this crippled thing couldn't have come so far.

Where had the other hoppers gone?

He wondered what had crippled this one. His own machine had done no more than sting it. He wondered if it had been hurt in the battle with Ben's ship.

Wondering, he almost forgot to be afraid.

Pushing at the rock with his stiff right fist, he moved closer to the hopper. He peered into the nearest yellow eye, wondering what the hopper was thinking about him. He saw the great eye shrink, as the shivering scales closed over it.

The hopper was afraid!

Suddenly a lot of things were clear to Jeff. Fear of men was the reason the hoppers had been waiting to fire at his ship, so far outside the ring of Topaz. Fear was the reason they had kept out of sight, baited their web with Ben's voice, and fired at every signal.

This hopper, he guessed, had been left to keep the web because it had been injured. All the others had fled. But here it was, three feet from the thing it feared, hurt and desperate, and he felt a little sorry for it.

He wished for a way to make peace with it. Perhaps if Buzz and Lupe were here . . .

But it was far too late for thoughts of peace. At least, Jeff knew, it was getting late for him. He caught himself yawning in the helmet. He could see the gray film of moisture spreading across the face plate, slowly shutting off his view. Dimly, he realized that the life support of his suit had been damaged in the fight.

Somehow he didn't care. He wanted to rip his helmet off, so that he could get one breath of good air, but he knew there was no air around him. For a long time he couldn't think of anything, except his need for air.

A pale red flicker reminded him of the hopper. He blinked through the fog on his face plate. He made out the cushion of black scales, the yellow eyes, the flashing laser.

But the great eyes weren't looking at him. They were staring off into the cloud. Following the red flash of its laser, Jeff found another huge rock. It was moving toward them, fast.

His old sense of mass and force and motion was working slowly now, but at last it told him why the hopper's laser was burning so wildly. It told him exactly where this new rock would strike the one where they were. He himself was safe, but the hopper wasn't.

It was going to be crushed between the rocks and it couldn't get out of the way. It was trying with its laser to break up the rock, but all of its power had been used. Jeff figured it had exactly twelve seconds left.

Jeff knew he ought to get farther back before the rock hit. He gripped a point of rock with his good left hand, to shove himself away. But something stopped him. He hung staring through his fogged face plate at the helpless, twisting hopper. Jeff knew he couldn't let it die.

Slowly, he moved toward it. The bright black scales pulled away from his gloves, shivering. The bright eye beneath him drew back into a slit. The dark laser turned toward him, glowing like a dying coal.

". . . caught . . ." A far ghost of Ben's voice whispered in his helmet. ". . . web . . ."

The hopper feared him more than it did the rushing rock. He knew it hated him. That dying whisper reminded him that it had trapped Ben's ship, possibly killed Ben and all his starmen. Yet he couldn't just watch it be crushed.

He caught it under a thick gray stump, with his left hand and his frozen fist. He drew a gasping breath of the bad air in his helmet and pulled.

The fat cushion moved a little, half sliding, and half rolling across the rock. Though it weighed almost nothing, here in the rocks, its mass was almost too much for him. He had to pull and pull again, and he hardly knew when it was safe.

Dimly, he felt his fist slip from under that flat stump, and the iron soles of his boots scrape across the face of the rock. He knew that he was lying where the rock would hit.

He tried to look for the hopper and the rock, but gray mist had filled all his face plate. He tried to breathe. His air was almost gone. He made an effort to move his body out of the way, a yard or a foot or just an inch, but his energy was used up.

What happened then was like a dim gray dream. He couldn't see what was going on, and he felt too weak and sick to care. But he thought one long silver arm had come back to the hopper. He thought he felt its quick tip whipping around his body to drag him from under that smashing rock.

"FIRST MAN TO TOPAZ"

IN HIS DREAM, Jeff was fighting to rescue Ben. He dived his jet suit into the ring around Topaz. He flew between rocks and searched through endless clouds. At last he came to the lost starship caught in the rock hopper's web.

Hot blue sparks stung him when he drew near the web. But he used his laser to cut the captured ship out of the web. He tore the coils from around the ship and opened the lock to look for Ben.

What he found was a yellow eye, bigger than his head, rimmed with shining scales. The hopper was waiting for him. A cold silver arm snaked out of the lock and whipped around his throat.

It choked him so that he couldn't breathe.

"Hi, Jeff." Ty's calm, strong voice called from somewhere. "Need some help?"

He opened his eyes. This wasn't a dream. It was real. Something covered his face. He tried to move, but his body was stiff and cold. A sharp pain stabbed through his head.

"Ty?" His voice was a dull croak. "Ty?"

His jet suit was gone. He couldn't remember where he was. He was shivering from a damp chill and fighting for breath.

"Take it easy, Jeff." Ty's easy voice was closer. "You'll be okay."

He tried to sit up, but he was wrapped in a thick cocoon of his own. Something hard and cold was strapped against his heart, and something stung his arms when he tried to move. A sharp sweet smell in the air burned his throat when he breathed.

"Easy, Jeff." Ty's voice was cheerful. "You are not supposed to wake up yet."

But he kept struggling until he felt something lifted from his head. Looking through a narrow slit in his bandages, he saw Ty's face floating over him. Ty was wearing dark glasses.

"I thought — " He had to stop and breathe, and the air hurt his lungs. "Thought the hoppers had me!"

"We've both been under deep sleep," Ty said. "I beat you out by a day and half. What they have to do to wake you up is not much fun, but Buzz says you'll be okay."

Jeff shook his pounding head to clear it. Peering through the slit, he recognized the padded metal shapes around him in the tall, round room. It was the cabin of his own ship. Too tired to be very much surprised at anything, he looked back at Ty.

"Your eyes?" he asked.

"Still weak," Ty said. "But I can see."

"I'm — glad!" He drew another breath. "How — how did I get here?"

"Buzz says the hoppers gave you a sleep shot from the aid kit in your own suit," Ty told him. "That kept you alive while they brought you out of the rocks."

"I was fighting a hopper — "

"But then you saved its life," Ty said. "Buzz didn't tell me how."

"I think I remember." He drew another long breath, which didn't hurt so much. "I remember a rock. I remember pushing the hopper out of the way."

"Buzz says that's why the hoppers helped you."

"What do they care?" He blinked through the slit. "They weren't acting very friendly when they trapped Ben's ship and copied his voice to bait a trap for us — "

"I will let you talk to Lupe," Ty said. "She knows more about it."

Ty disappeared. Alone in the room, Jeff closed his aching eyes to rest them. When he looked up again, Lupe was bending over him.

"Don't worry, Jeff." Her cool hand felt good on his hot forehead. "You are trying to wake up too soon."

"I want to know about the hoppers," he told her.

"They were afraid," she said. "You see, all the hoppers belong to one great being — a queer, vast

115

creature that is even stranger than Buzz's multiple mind. Each hopper has parts that can be separate beings or work together as they choose. But all the hoppers share one common intelligence, as Buzz and all his brother-sisters do. Their mind is the only one in all the rings of Topaz. It had never met another mind. That's why it was afraid."

Jeff tried to understand.

"Buzz had crawled back into his cocoon as we drifted toward the ring," she said. "He had sensed the hopper mind, and he was trying hard to make contact. The hopper mind was closed to him because it was afraid. But when you risked your own life to save that hopper, its mind saw that we could be friends. It opened up to Buzz."

"So now the hoppers are our friends?"

"They're Buzz's friends, anyhow." Her face came closer. "His mind has a lot in common with theirs. Buzz has been telling me all about them."

"What are they like?" His voice stopped when he remembered the mystery and wonder of the hoppers. "How can they exist? Out among these dry, bare, flying rocks, with no planet at all!"

"Buzz says they're as strange and wonderful as human beings are." A quick smile lighted her face. "He says the working of their bodies is based on metals, the way ours is based on water."

"So they really eat rocks!"

"Buzz says they do eat certain ones. They drink hot metal. They don't have to breathe. Their bodies produce electric and magnetic forces, as well as laser beams. They fly with natural jets."

"Queer things!"

"Buzz says we seem queer to them. The air we breathe would burn them up."

"I guess in a way we're odd, too." Jeff moved stiffly in his tight cocoon. "But how do they live? Do they have machines and ships and cities?"

"Buzz says they have no use for things like that. Their bodies don't need them. Their great common mind keeps them all in touch, so they don't have to crowd into cities."

"What do they *do*?"

"They live," she said. "They weave their homes of metal strands. They spread their webs to gather food. They have their families and bring up the new-born hoppers. Buzz says their family webs are scattered far apart, wherever they can find the rare ores they need for food."

"Is that all?" Jeff felt somehow disappointed. "For things like the hoppers, that seems — well, dull."

Lupe shook her head.

"They think," she said. "They feel. Their rocks are filled with treasures and with dangers. They have to search all through the ring for the ores they eat. They have to hide from terrible creatures that prey on them."

Resting in his firm cocoon, Jeff tried to picture that.

"Sometimes, Buzz says, they leave their rocks. They

swarm out into open space. They drift down toward Topaz, soaking up the energy of its rays the way our green plants do. The pure bright light makes them happy. They fly through patterns like dances and sing songs of silent thought."

Jeff looked up at Lupe, trying hard to understand.

"Maybe they aren't so dull," he said. "Anyway, I'm glad they're our friends."

"They do want to be," she said. "They saved your life, when they gave you that sleep shot and brought you back to the probe. They even made new parts for the boosters, when Buzz taught them how, so that we can fly the ship again. They want to help us get back home."

"Why?" he asked.

"Because now they see that we will help them, when they help us. Buzz says they'd always been afraid of life on other stars. Now they want to join us."

"That's great," he said. "But when can I get up?"

"Not yet," Lupe said. "You have two more shots to take before we can get you up."

He felt too weak to object when he saw the bright needle in her hand. He woke feeling better. The stiff bandages were gone so that he could move. Lupe helped him sit up. He sat for a moment rubbing the small blue scars on his left arm, where tubes had been attached. They were healed almost smooth.

"Ty and Buzz are up in the cockpit," Lupe told

him. "We are circling outside the ring, not far from your brother's ship. Buzz is having a wonderful time talking to the hopper mind."

"What about — about Ben?" Jeff looked hard at Lupe, afraid of what she would say. "Is he alive?"

She shook her head. "I don't know. Buzz doesn't either."

"Why were the hoppers fighting him, if they want to be so friendly now?"

"They thought his laser was a weapon," Lupe said. "You see, they don't talk with their own lasers. They have a better link through their common mind. They use their own lasers just for tools — for blasting rock and fusing ore. When Ben began to signal, they thought he was trying to destroy them."

"What did they do to him?"

"They fought to keep him out of the ring," Lupe said. "Ben fought back. When he got close enough, he did use his laser for a weapon. He hurt the hopper you found, before they caught his ship in the web."

"But that was all before we made peace," Jeff said. "Won't they help him now?"

"Ty and Buzz have been trying to persuade them to do something," Lupe said. "But they haven't made peace with Ben. They're still afraid of him. They won't go near the ship in the web."

"Then we are going after Ben," Jeff said. "That's why we came to Topaz."

"We are ready," Lupe said, "as soon as you feel up

to it. Ty has been repairing your jet suit with new parts the hoppers made for him. Buzz says the hoppers will guide us back."

"I'm okay," Jeff said. "Let's go."

Eagerly, he climbed ahead of her to the cockpit. He felt weak at first, but he didn't want to wait. They found Ty sleeping in one of the seats with the dark glasses over his eyes.

"He's not strong yet," Lupe whispered. "But he's getting better."

Buzz was in the pilot's seat. He looked too small for it, but his short fur was bright gold with happiness. He was sucking at a thick yellow tube.

"Gear grease," Lupe explained. "He loves it."

Buzz wiped his lips and carefully licked his hand. Blinking his green eyes, he whistled at Jeff.

"He and Ty have everything ready," Lupe said. "The hoppers are waiting to guide us."

"Let's go," Jeff said.

Buzz purred and stretched to reach the control board with his small paws. The ship swung toward the blazing ring. Buzz kept chirping as they flew.

"He's still talking to the hopper mind," Lupe said. "He's telling it all about X-space flight. The hoppers have found the parts of the two stations they wrecked. Buzz is telling them how to use the parts to make a new station for Topaz. He says the hoppers want to open X-space to us. They have plenty of metals to trade, and we have many things to offer them."

"So the hoppers are coming to Earth?"

Jeff was thinking of that cabman back on Earth who didn't like Buzz. When the hoppers came, he thought, the people of Earth would have to learn to get along with stranger life than Buzz.

Even to him, the hoppers were still frightening. He couldn't help an odd feeling when one of them came flying to meet their ship. Yet he knew that it was now a friend. He knew that it had come to guide them to Ben, and he began to feel the excitement of learning about such a different way of life.

This hopper had been joined by another part which pushed it through open space. The extra part was a dark cone that fitted under the flat black body between the coiled silver arms. The tip of the cone shone with changing shades of blue as the hopper turned and moved. Jeff thought the cone must be a kind of living jet.

As they followed the hopper into the ring, shattered rocks whirled around them. Deep inside the dim blue cloud they came to the beaded web where Ben's ship was caught. Jeff squeezed into his jet suit and flew down.

The locks were blocked with the bright coils of the web, but that didn't matter. He found a hole big enough for him where a laser bolt had ripped through the skin of the ship.

The cabin was empty of air and very cold. The green glow of his laser machine picked out Jim Ozaki and Tony Mescalero, lying side by side against the

cabin wall. Their bodies were stiff. He thought they were dead until he saw the dim red glow of the timers on their wrists.

He bent to read the timers. MAN UNDER DEEP SLEEP, the red letters said. MUST BE AWAKENED BEFORE TIME RUNS OUT. Both timers had been set for one thousand hours. Both showed that nine hundred and ninety-seven hours had passed.

Jeff hoped he had not come too late. Hurrying on to look for Ben, he found Whiz Miller in the back of the ship, where another bolt had chopped the main power cables. His timer was set like the others.

Jeff climbed to the cockpit, searching for Ben. In the green glow of his light, he saw Ben's face. The blue eyes were open, but the flesh looked cold.

He found the broken needle stuck through the sleeve of the jet suit into Ben's frozen arm. The timer was not buckled to his wrist, but tossed on the instrument board. Set for one thousand hours, it showed that Ben had thirteen hours left.

That small red timer told the story. Ben had fought on, ten hours longer, after his men had taken deep sleep. He had fought on until his laser was dead.

Jeff called his ship.

"Ben and his men are all in deep sleep. They need help — now!"

"Stand by," Ty's voice came back. "Buzz says the hoppers will help you move your brother and his starmen."

The hoppers didn't need a signal, because Buzz

now had a link to their common mind. They came out of the rocks around the web. Their flat black bodies and their yellow eyes still made Jeff feel a bit strange, but their quick silver arms lifted the sleeping starmen with a wonderful strength and care.

Back on their starship, Jeff and Ty stripped the men, handling them carefully with thick gloves. They were cold as liquid air. In the warm cabin, white feathers of frost grew all around them.

Buzz examined each of them, his big green eyes very solemn. He took a long time over Ben, in silent contact with the multiple mind of his race.

"He says we are late," Lupe spoke for him. "He says we will have to warm them very carefully in the packs before we do anything else. He doesn't know just what effect this much cold will have."

Their stiff bodies didn't fit the shock seats. Jeff and Ty strapped them into hammocks hung across the cabin. Jeff helped Lupe wrap them in the thick packs and watched Buzz strap the pacemakers over their hearts.

"That's all we can do until they are thawed," Lupe said. "Then we can start the shots and connect the machine to wash the deep sleep drugs out of their blood. When they begin breathing, we can start the oxygen."

"When will we know if they are alive?"

"Not for hours." She gave him a searching look. "You are worn out, Jeff. You haven't gotten over your own deep sleep. Better take a nap."

He complained, but when Ty had gone back to the cockpit and Lupe was watching the sleeping men and he had nothing to do, he lay back in an empty shock seat to rest for just a moment. The next thing he knew, Ty was shaking him.

"Wake up, Jeff. You've slept twelve hours."

He sat up with a start and looked around the cabin. The hammocks were gone, but he saw one man wrapped up in the seat across from him, still attached to the black tubes.

"That's your brother," Ty said. "The others came out of it hours ago. Tony Mescalero's up in the cockpit now, spelling me. Jim and Whiz went back to the other ship. The hoppers are helping them fix it up. They mean to fly it back to the moon."

"That's fine," Jeff said, without feeling anything. He got out of the seat and bent over the sleeping man. "How's Ben?"

"We don't know yet," Ty said. "Buzz says the deep sleep needle was broken off in his arm. He didn't quite get a full shot of the drug. His body may have been damaged. We just don't know."

Jeff watched until he couldn't sit still any longer. He climbed into the cockpit and found Tony Mescalero on the phone. Tony grinned and shook his hand and let him speak to the other ship.

With the hoppers' help, Jim Ozaki and Whiz Miller had finished the repairs and moved their ship out of the rocks. They wanted Tony to join them now. Jeff took the controls and circled back to meet them. Flying slowly between the dead black sky and the ring of Topaz, he waited for news of Ben.

No news had come when the two starships met. Tony went out in his jet suit and flew across to meet the other ship. Five rock hoppers helped the two ships move away from the ring, picking a safe path between the clouds of dust. They danced ahead, floating and darting, and finally flew back to their world of rocks.

Jeff twisted in his seat and waited for news.

Why, he wondered, had he never been content to let Ben be first at anything? How could he ever have envied his own brother?

He heard Lupe on the ladder behind him.

His voice caught. "How's Ben?"

"We still don't know," she said. "But Buzz has a message for you. From Admiral Serov on the moon."

In a different voice, she recited the message.

"To Starman Jefferson Stone. My personal regards to you and the starmen with you. I hope your brother recovers, and we are keeping your parents informed. We are happy about the success of your mission. We are glad to welcome the rock hoppers into our great family."

She asked if he wanted to answer. He told her he would wait until he knew about Ben. She came back later to say that Ben was doing well. "He's awake," she told him. "You can go in to see him now."

"Well, kid!" Ben gripped Jeff's hand with his

old strength. His face looked pale, but his blue eyes had their familiar bright shine. "I never expected to see you here."

They talked about the flights from Earth and the battle with the hoppers. Ben asked about their parents.

"You know Mom," Jeff said.

"When I signed up for the Topaz flight," Ben said, "I wasn't worried about her and Dad. Or even about finding new facts for science or new worlds for men. All I really had in mind was just to be the first man to Topaz."

"And I had to follow," Jeff said. "Because I wanted to catch up."

"Glad you did." Ben grinned and punched Jeff on the shoulder, but in a moment his face was grave again. "You know, kid, in a way that fight with the hoppers was all my fault."

"Buzz said they didn't understand you — "

"But I wasn't even trying to understand them," Ben said. "You see, they didn't attack me at first. They just fired bolts ahead of me to warn me, trying to keep me out of their ring. But I came on in spite of them."

"Look!" Jeff was staring at the dusty dark ahead. "Out there!"

There in the dark, far toward the distant sun and its small Earth, an orange spark burned and went out. A green spark lit —

"That's the new beacon!" Jeff whispered. "Out at the new station. The hoppers have put it together. The way to Earth is open again."

Ty went up to take the controls. Buzz was hopping ahead of him, purring happily and sucking at a new tube of grease. Jeff and Ben asked him to have his sister-brother on the moon let their parents know that they were well.

Buzz chirped and nodded.

When Jeff and Ben went up to the cockpit, Lupe was flying the ship. Buzz was in his cocoon, she said, and Ty had gone across to take command of the other starship. When Lupe got up, Jeff waited for Ben to move into the pilot's seat.

"Take over, Jeff," Ben waved him ahead. "You've come a long way. I think it's your turn now. Fly us back to the beacon."

Jeff grinned and took the pilot's seat. After a last look back toward the ring of Topaz, he flashed a signal to Ty in the ship behind and steered for the winking beacon.